Tis the Season for a *Cowboy*

A SMALL TOWN HOLIDAY NOVELLA

AVA HUNTER

ALSO BY AVA HUNTER

Aisle of Paradise Series
Babymoon or Bust
For Better or Hearse

Runaway Ranch Series
Tame the Heart
Rope the Moon
Burn the Wild
Ride the Sky

Nashville Star Series
Sing You Home
Find You Again
Love You Always
Need You Now
Bring You Back
With You Forever

TROPES

Divorced couple, second chance, snowed in, cowboy, forced proximity, small town, marriage in crisis.

TRIGGERS

This book features the mention of stillbirth, flashbacks of pregnancy loss, and dealing with grief.

If any of these trigger you, please skip this book.

CONTENT WARNINGS

This book contains profane language and explicit sexual scenes.

'Tis the Season for a Cowboy

1

Bellamy

"**M**OM, STOP." ONE EYE ON THE ROAD IN FRONT OF me, I fumble with the radio dial.

The rental car zigzags briefly across the yellow center line, and I curse as Bing Crosby's "White Christmas" fades out.

"I'll be fine. I swear it."

"You swear, but you also lie, Bell Bug." There's a sigh on the other end of the line. "Are you sure this is a good idea?"

No. I'm not sure it's a good idea. I've flown one thousand miles and spent money I don't have, and for what? To hole myself up in a cabin in the frigid Montana wilderness for ninety-six hours in hopes that I'll paint something good enough to salvage my career? Yes. That's exactly what I plan to do.

But I don't say any of that to my mom.

"It's your thirtieth birthday *and* Christmas. You shouldn't be alone to—to wallow."

"I'm not wallowing. I'm painting." My chest squeezes as the words leave me.

The confidence I had when I left San Francisco has already dissipated. The parting words my agent, Luka, left me with linger in my head.

Try to paint something we can sell this time.

"And that cabin will help you, how?" A psychiatrist, my mother loves to poke at open wounds. Even if it's all in the best interest of her only child.

"I still love it there." I rub at the ache between my brows. "Despite what happened."

I'm in a drought. The cabin's always been a source of inspiration. With any luck, I can reclaim that this Christmas. If not, I can kiss my career goodbye.

"Okay," my mother decides. I can almost see her mime locking her lips. "Not another word. Next Christmas you're mine."

A wave of warm affection rolls through me. "Promise."

Once I've ended the call, I vow not to pick my phone up for the rest of the year. Unless it's Luka calling with life-changing news. My mom knows exactly what this time of the year does to me, but I'm nowhere near ready to get into that therapy session.

"Hot cocoa. A fireplace. A fresh paint set. And the

biggest, butteriest blanket I can find," I murmur, doing my best to convince myself that this idea is a great big present topped with a beautiful red bow and not a lump of coal stuck in the bottom of my stocking.

Christmas in Montana.

After two hellish plane rides, with turbulence violent enough to give me whiplash, and three hours stuck in a horrible, smelly rental car, I'm ready for it.

I love Christmas.

I love everything that comes with the magical holiday season. Eggnog and hot toddies. Red stockings and silver twinkling lights. A freshly cut tree (never fake) and powdered snow. The roar of the fire. Sugar cookies with buttercream frosting. Mistletoe and cozy sweaters. Cinnamon rolls on Christmas morning and Irish coffee in the afternoon. Long, lazy days and even lazier nights.

Even after all that's happened.

Maybe because some dumb, idealistic part of me clings to the belief that miracles can come true, clings to those last few days of the year when all is bright white and hopeful.

I inhale, sit up straighter and turn up the radio. As Elvis Presley's slow croon of "Blue Christmas" fills the car, a faint flicker of Christmas spirit spreads through me. A hint of a happy sensation I haven't felt in the last three years.

Elvis continues his serenade as I ease off the highway and enter Silverwood. The quintessential land of cowboys with its red-bricked buildings, annual rodeos and busy saloons. I let off the gas and survey Main Street mournfully. The little downtown that I once truly loved as my own is decorated with wreaths and shiny garland. I ache to stop, to step into Candy's Candy Shop for hand-pulled taffy, snag a gingerbread cookie from Baked or a Silverwood Amber Ale from Buck's Bar.

Instead, speed limit be damned, I accelerate.

The bruise in my heart throbs.

Silverwood isn't my town. I left.

I don't deserve it.

As I put the familiar buildings in my rearview, I swallow the knot in my throat. Maybe I should have let Hank have the cabin this year. Maybe I should have stayed in San Francisco and put in overtime at the gallery. Maybe I should have rethought every decision I've made in the last three years.

Soon, I follow the twisty road up, up, up. High above the jagged mountain in front of me loom tall, dark clouds. Though the ground is clear of snow for now, those clouds say *just wait*. Silverwood is known for its infamous Christmas blizzards, so I need to get to my destination fast.

When the road forks to a narrow dirt road, I turn right. As the rental car bumps along, the familiar signs that guide folks toward the Blue Mountain Ranch and Christmas Tree Farm dot my periphery, looking dingier than usual. I make a note to send Hank a sternly worded text message, instructing him to clean them up for next season.

Hank.

My stomach twists into a knot of nerves at the thought of my ex-husband. With another deep breath, I remind myself that he's safely on the other side of the ranch with the animals. There's no reason to think I'll run into him. He knows it's my year.

According to the cabin custody clause we worked out in our divorce contract.

Hank got it the first year.

Then me.

Though we agreed to alternate years, we made a little adjustment when we came to the arrangement. On my thirtieth birthday, I get it.

I may have walked away from the ranch and from the town I loved, but I couldn't give up my cabin.

Everything else, we divvied up as fairly as we could. He kept the ranch and the tree farm and the dog. I got the car and our small savings.

At the time, arguing and dividing up assets patched the gaping hole in us, but nothing will ever fix what we lost.

After another mile, I finally break through the trees. And there, in the middle of a shimmering emerald pine forest, is a bright red barn.

Blue Mountain Christmas Tree Farm. A choose-and-cut farm that's been a staple in Silverwood for more than fifty years.

I break into a true smile for the first time in what feels like forever, though I quickly tamp down on the excitement stirring inside me. This isn't home. Not anymore. And I have to remember that.

The scene is straight from a Hallmark card. Two massive Clydesdales—Bonnie and Clyde—haul a tree on a sled, their bells jingling, while customers stand nearby, watching with bright smiles. The lights and the plastic candy canes that line a path to the Christmas tree farm are testaments to the Blue way. Year after year, they make Christmas magical for every customer.

The air goes out of me when I see Silas "Papa" Blue, Hank's father, stepping out of the barn, hand on the brim of his Stetson. It makes sense that he's here; he owns the farm, after all. But suddenly, I'm hit with the inexplicable urge to break down and cry.

Before I can punch the gas and roll by, he spots me, his head lifting. So I brake gently and turn the wheel with white knuckles, gliding into a makeshift parking spot.

You can do this, Bellamy. Dry your eyes first, then stiffen your body.

I exit the car and drink in the scent of Fraser fir, concolor fir, and white pine. A gust of wind whispers through the trees, ruffling my hair and sending goose bumps erupting along my skin. The sun dips lower as I follow the footpath up to the barn to meet Papa Blue.

"I wouldn't believe it if I didn't see it." He's a little less athletic than Hank, and his cowboy hat is dusty, as always. The man is physically incapable of spending time indoors, no matter the weather. "Bellamy Blue here to stay."

I ignore his craggy smirk and the use of that last name. He's correct anyway. It hasn't changed.

Curling my arms around him, I sink into his strong hug and sigh. He smells like pipe and apple cider. "Not stay. You know that, Pops."

He makes a sound of dubious refusal in the back of his throat, releasing me. "What are you doin' in town then?"

"It's my year for the cabin." I brush a strand of hair from my face. "My thirtieth."

"That so?" His eyes widen, then he chuckles. "Must have forgot."

I lift my chin and survey the farm. Nearby, an employee hands a little girl a candy cane. A mitten-clad couple buys cups of peppermint hot chocolate from a food truck.

Mouth watering, I turn back to my former father-in-law. "How's the farm? Business looks booming."

"It's keepin' on." His brow furrows, thick fingers hooking into his belt loops. "How 'bout you, honey?"

"Oh, you know," I say, forcing a smile, "doing the same."

"You good?" His question is gruff, but Papa Blue always listened to me in a way that no one else could. He saw everything, even if he didn't say so.

No, I'm not good. That's what I want to say. I want to tell him that I miss Silverwood and our Christmas tree farm. That I hate my job in the city.

I always wanted to be an artist, but I wanted Hank more, so I traded big city life in San Francisco for a slow-paced one in small-town Montana. Four years into our marriage, I painted a piece inspired by Hank, titled it, *Cowboy Wading into Water* and posted it on Instagram. It blew up overnight, and I became known for my distinctive Montana scenes. I was even featured in Target's Artist Spotlight series.

It was a beautiful burst of glory I haven't recaptured since.

After the divorce, I went back to the art gallery I left when I met Hank. While I worked the front desk, I put together my portfolio. Networked.

My agent organized a gallery show, but instead of

hitting it big again, I failed. Spectacularly. I only sold one painting that night. After, in my quiet, dark apartment, I cried and typed out a text I never sent.

Rather than dive into any of that, I plaster on a smile. "Good."

Papa Blue peers at me. "Still living that artist life?"

"Pretty close."

Starving artist is more like it.

"Honey, you're living in an apartment the size of a cardboard box," my mom loves to remind me every time we talk. "Use your divorce settlement."

But I can't. I don't know why. Using that money feels like admitting that I've given up. But on what? I still don't know. Myself? Hank and me? That's ridiculous. There is no more *Hank and me*. I'm twenty-nine and divorced. That's the epitome of giving up.

A harsh gust of icy wind whips through the trees. I hitch a thumb at my rental car. "I should get up to the cabin before the storm blows in."

"Car won't make it up that incline." Papa Blue's gaze narrows in disapproval.

Over my shoulder, I eye the shoddy Kia and curse the rental company.

I blink at him. "What do I do?"

He grins, the lines on his face deepening. "You can still pull a sled, can't you?"

Ten minutes later, my bags are stacked on top of a rustic red Christmas sled and the clouds in the sky have lowered further.

He gives the sled, then me, a doubtful look. "You need help up?"

I puff a lock of hair out of my face. "It's okay. I got it." Balancing my backpack on my thigh, I dig a pair of thick gloves out and slide them on.

"Still a natural." Papa Blue breaks into a proud grin.

I smile. A real one this time.

"You give a holler if you need anything." He squeezes my arm. "We missed you around these parts. Don't be a stranger."

I ignore the *we*. And the pressure behind my eyes. "I won't. Thanks."

Slowly, I leave behind the buzzing Christmas tree farm and hoof my way up the steep incline. It's only a ten-minute trek, but already my ass muscles burn. Luckily, the hills of San Francisco have prepared me for this.

As I ascend, I hum "Jingle Bells" and periodically peer up at the thick black clouds that have moved in.

"Almost there," I huff as I weave through thick pine trees, my boots crunching leaves and rock. When the top of the A-frame cabin peeks through the dark treetops like a guiding light, my heart stutters.

Once the ground flattens out, I shove my way through the forest, passing the hand-carved sign that reads *Our Mansion in the Mountains*.

That's what Hank and I called it.

It may only be eight hundred square feet, but we lived so many dreamy moments here and created so many happy memories. My first sale. A call from an agent. The night Hank and I first made love. The start of what became our traditional Christmas tree ornament exchange. The time Hank and I—

A lone snowflake lands on my nose, snapping me back into focus.

Stop.

Stop thinking about Hank.

He doesn't matter. He isn't here.

The tightness in my chest eases when the cabin comes fully into view. Surrounded by a small grove of trees, it gleams like a Christmas oasis. Snowflake wind chimes dangle, clinking lightly, from a frosted eave. The wide front porch with its green front door. A pyramid of firewood perfectly stacked. Festive glittery lights strung along the sloped roof.

For what feels like the first time in three years, a surge of joy overtakes me. To me, this cabin is home. It's always been home.

I move quicker this time, out of hope, out of happy, patting my front pocket to ensure my key is ready. My body purrs at the sleep I plan to catch up on. My fingers itch to paint until I've gone Van Gogh. My mouth waters in anticipation of the food I plan to eat, ready to tuck into life-changing carbohydrates like it's a matter of life or death. Two strides from the front porch, a loud hacking sound hits my ears.

Going stock still, like a doe scenting danger, I scan my surroundings. Someone's on the property. Someone's on *my* property.

I steel a breath, yank off my gloves and wedge my key between my thumb and forefinger like a claw. Then, leaving the sled, I hustle around the cabin, prepared to give the trespasser a piece of my mind. Because peace *from* my mind is what I desperately need these next few days.

But, as I stumble through the trees, I forget my bearings. I haven't been here in over a year. I trip over a tree stump and run smack dab into a Fraser fir.

Then a shock of olive-green flannel. A hard body. A thunderous grunt.

I look up.

Oh God. My worst nightmare.

My ex-husband.

2

Bellamy

"B ELLAMY?"

I freeze at the voice. That fucking rough, gravelly voice that still haunts my dreams.

Hank straightens, big hands clenched around an axe. Below him is a tree stump. On top of that, a split log that looks comically small in comparison to Hank's wildly tall frame.

I jump back, putting much-needed space between us. "Jesus, Hank."

Every emotion I own pools in my belly like warm honey. I hate it. It feels like a thousand years since I left Hank, since we signed divorce papers, but the man is still as unfairly handsome as ever. With his golden-brown hair and deep sapphire eyes, Hank Blue is one dreamboat of a cowboy.

"What are you doing here?"

One brow rockets straight up on his rugged face. "Me?"

"Yes. You." I frown when I notice that, despite the windchill, he stubbornly wears a cowboy hat and a lone flannel in lieu of a jacket.

The scruff on his face is new. Not quite a beard, but effortless laziness, like he can't be bothered to shave. A few more faint crinkles line the corner of his eyes.

I like both.

My core tightens.

A muscle jerks in his jaw. He looks down at the chopping block, his broad shoulders lowering. I bet he wishes that log was my head.

"What."

Chop.

"Are."

Chop.

"You."

Chop.

"Doing."

Chop.

"Here?"

Through his many manly frustrated grunts, he doesn't look up. Not once.

He's not happy to see me. Why would he be? Three years ago, we shattered to pieces, and I left him. If I were him, I wouldn't forgive me either. But that doesn't mean I have to take his surly attitude.

"It's my Christmas."

He lifts his head, hits me with one of his familiar, exasperated looks. "Your Christmas to what?"

"To stay at the cabin."

Now, he lifts the axe.

I flinch.

With an under-his-breath mutter of "for Christ's sakes," he sets it aside. "It's my Christmas, Bell. My cabin."

I dig in my boots. "We both own the cabin. It's in the contract. *And* it's my weekend." When he stares at me, I snort.

"Unbelievable. You forgot." Sighing, I tip my head back and study the snow now falling from fat gray clouds.

Hank Blue never forgets a damn thing.

But why would he remember this? It's not his job. Not anymore.

"It's my thirtieth birthday." I face him beneath the trees as the Montana wind steals its way beneath my thick parka. "We agreed I could stay here, remember? In the divorce?"

"Fuck." Hard gaze softening, he drags a hand down the whiskers of his jaw.

He opens his mouth to say something. What, I'm not sure, because before he can speak, my knees go out from under me.

A pair of paws lands on my chest. A red, drooly tongue drags its way down my chin.

"Oh my God!" I gape at the furry face, then propel myself up and fling my arms around the blue heeler.

She wriggles, panting against my neck, but I hold on tight as joy zips through me. "Zelda, girl! My sweet, silly mashed potato pup."

She was a gift for Hank, for Christmas the first year we were married. With one brown eye and one blue, she's adorable, but the goofy underbite that makes her look like she has a perpetual grin is what made me scream "she's mine" when she was a tiny puppy. The instant I saw her wiggling and squirming with her siblings, I had to have her. And looking at her now, I can't believe I ever left her.

"Oh, I missed you," I whisper into her thick scruff.

After she's given me a few more sloppy forehead kisses, I press my hands into the cold earth and push my way to standing.

She sticks to my side, her tail thwacking against the side of my leg.

"Hell, what are we goin' to do about this?" Hank considers me, blue eyes searching my face. Serious. Assessing. Always working out problems in that marvel of a brain of his.

Me, I was quick to act, to react.

I eye the cabin steps, wanting nothing more than to dramatically storm up them and slam the front door in his face.

Instead, I blow out a puff of breath, shivering in the biting cold. "We are not doing anything. You're going and I'm staying. Simple as that."

With a toss of my hair, I turn away. *There. That should do it.*

I've only taken two steps before Hank's boots crunch

leaves and gravel beside me. Zelda trots ahead, lunging for snowflakes, snapping and biting.

He scoffs, breath a white cloud in front of him. "You can't just show up here and tell me to go."

"That's exactly what I'm doing." I look around for his vintage Bronco. Why didn't I see it before?

All I find is a junky rusted truck nestled in a grove of trees.

I chance a glance at him in my periphery and see it. That jaw set in stone. The little line between his eyes that he gets when he does the crossword or fixes a saddle.

It makes me move faster. "You live just over the ridge. It'll take you minutes to get home. I spent eight hours on a plane, then three more in a rental car. I can't just pack up and leave." Not to mention I have a bed and a bottle of wine calling my name.

Key out, I reach for my bags, but before I can grasp a handle, Hank hauls them into his arms. Without a word, he stomps past me up the stairs and throws open the door.

"You don't have to do that." I follow him, watching grudgingly as he carries my bags into the cabin.

Zelda bounds behind us frantically, as if she doesn't know what to think of my appearance.

"Already done." Hank drops my bags onto the floor without flourish.

I cross fast over the threshold, refusing to look up at the silver star-shaped mistletoe hook hanging above. Even so, I tense at the visceral reaction, at the memories that careen through me.

Waiting for Hank on Christmas Day for our mistletoe

kiss. The tree farm was closed, and cider simmered on the stove. The scent was strong in the air, though suddenly, it was joined by the harsh tang of blood.

Breath hitching painfully, I look down at my stomach. "Bell?"

Hank watches me, his brow knitted in concern.

It's then that I catch my reflection in the mirror hanging near the entryway and understand why. The bags under my eyes are heavier than those he just lugged inside for me. My dark windswept hair could host a family of rats, and my sweater hangs off my body courtesy of the fantastic combination of stress and depression.

I look like a winter crone.

"I'm fine," I say before he can ask.

My attention drifts. To the cabin. Picture-perfect charm.

Unlike the cowboy glowering beside me.

A dusty mahogany-colored leather couch faces the rock-wall fireplace. Above the mantel, an oil-painting of the ranch during winter. Nestled in a corner, two mismatched chairs and a small table meant for games and cozying up with books on a neighboring bookshelf. The kitchen's tiny, tucked away between exposed wood beams. A butcher block island, hunter-green cabinets, shelves and hooks make the most of the space. Across from the kitchen, a ladder that leads up to a loft.

The place is moody and rustic, making me want to hole myself up for the holidays.

The joy of seeing the cabin evaporates in an instant, and I frown, watching as Hank sets his hat on the coffee table, watching as he shakes the chill from his lean frame and wanders to the wood burning stove for warmth.

My stomach drops when I see his bags strewn around the house. His things are everywhere. A crossword puzzle book. A nonfiction paperback about Wyatt Earp. A bottle of whiskey. Coffee cups everywhere because Hank's MO has always been pouring five cups of coffee a day and never finishing any of them. Zelda's tattered dog bed propped in a corner.

Shit. He's unpacked. Made himself at home.

This absolutely cannot happen.

Standing beneath the warm glow of the cabin light, it's hard not to take him in. I've always been attracted to the man. A divorce won't change that fact. His golden-brown hair's tousled and messy, curled at the nape. Longer than I'm used to. Those long legs, that ass are stacked with muscle. The corded veins in his thick forearms run down to big, tan working man's hands.

Hands.

That's when I see it. My mind squirrels.

"Hank." My heart flutters. Ignoring the traitorous little organ, I set my hands on my hips. The best disappointed ex-wife move I can muster. "Your ring."

"It won't come off." He grunts, steamrolling over my protest. He lifts a tan hand, causing the silver band to flash in the firelight. "Gained too much weight."

Liar. I narrow my eyes at his hard, post-divorce vengeance body. Gained too much muscle is far more likely.

I blink away the thought. I won't dig into what it means. Don't want to. Don't care.

"Hank." Frustration simmers in my veins. I don't want to spend my Christmas fighting. I don't want to spend my Christmas with *him*. "You need to go."

"Stop telling me to leave, Bell." His voice is low, rough.

"We both can't stay here," I remind him quietly. I cross my arms, digging my fingers into my biceps. "Please, Hank. I need this."

He peers at me, his blue eyes full of questions, like he's looking for an answer in the memory of my face. Then, after a resigned sigh, he moves through the house, collecting his bags. As he meanders closer, I catch a whiff of his scent. Coffee and pine and horses.

There's that ache again. Stomach. Heart. Thighs.

He's leaving. Good. As relieved as I am, I'm also sad about it. A fact that pisses me off.

Time flies, but it feels like I was in that bar with my cowboy only yesterday.

That night, I watched the cowboys.

Thanks to a flight delay, I was stuck in the middle-of-nowhere Montana. I ventured out of my hotel and went to the locals' bar on Main Street. Buck's Bar. I parked myself at a high-top with my sketch pad and a vodka soda. It's said inspiration is found in the strangest of places, and for me, that place was Silverwood. It wasn't my usual scene, but the view was spectacular.

I watched as dusty and rough-around-the edges cowboys played pool. Blushed when they called me ma'am. Their casual hat tips altered my heart's beat.

When the bells over the door jingled, I twisted in my seat. My gaze snagged on a man who looked like no one I'd ever gone for before. Six foot three, tall, rugged. Chiseled jaw, intense eyes. I shamelessly stared.

He was a walking heartbreak in a chambray shirt and brown Stetson.

His boots were sharp across the sawdust floor. The way he worked the crowd, slapping backs, buying drinks, told me he was a regular.

When the cowboy settled at the bar with a group of friends, I leaned low on the table, resting my chin on my forearms, and drank him in. I preferred to sketch with pencils, but this man? He could convince me to get out the clay and sculpt. I wanted to document every beautiful detail.

Pulling out a pen, I tore my gaze from the handsome stranger and sketched him quickly. Biceps, belt buckle, and those bright blue eyes. When I was finished, I tipped back the last of my drink. Considered my options. That pulse down below.

It had been a while and I was feeling brave, if not horny. So I tore the page from my sketch pad and headed his way. I'd always been one for knee-jerk, for snap decisions. Maybe it was the artist in me. Never wanting to settle, hating to wait. Tonight wasn't any different.

I slid his sketch across the bar top and looked him in the eyes. "Sure look good in those Wranglers, cowboy."

He laughed, and the sound lit me up. Bright and deep and bold. Like he'd been happy all his life. He took me in, attention raking down the off-the-shoulder sweater and ripped jeans I'd tossed on before leaving my motel room.

"That's a hell of a line, sugar." His face changed to a serious earnestness as he studied the drawing. "Hell of a drawing too."

"I'm an artist." I pinched my fingers together. "Only minimally starving."

Another beautiful laugh. A shiver rolled down my spine.

"Hank Blue." He held out a big hand.

Heat snapped between us as his rough, calloused palm pressed into mine. I committed the feel to memory. "Well, Hank Blue, I'm Bellamy."

"Buy you a drink?" He stood, carefully folding, then tucking the drawing into his back pocket.

The gentleness with which he did so made me shiver.

A crooked grin overtook his face as he glanced back at his snickering friends. "Away from these animals."

Hank claimed a high-top and I sat on the stool next to him. We drank whiskey and bonded over the loss of a parent, the feral joy-rage that possessed us when working to beat the New York Times crossword puzzle and our shared passion for Christmas.

"It has to be a real tree." I waved my drink around like it was a gavel. Hiccupped. "Every day of the week."

He set his glass on the table with a thud. "Hell, if you don't find a live animal livin' in it, you've gone wrong."

I laughed, and it was like wildflowers blooming inside my heart.

"Now the real question," I said, "is lights. White or multicolored?"

"Multicolored."

Head tilted, I pressed my lips together. "Hmm. I prefer white."

"Ain't a deal-breaker, is it, sugar?" Hank's heated gaze slid to me and held.

"No." I bit my lip, heat flooding me in response to the nickname. "It's not."

"So, city girl, you find a lot of live trees in San Francisco?" He ran a hand over his sharp jaw.

I studied him, like I could memorize every beautiful angle.

"I try." Leg dancing under the table, I propped my cheek in my palm. "It bother you? I'm not a country girl?" I went for flirty, even though my question was genuine. What type of girl would this man go for?

But my effort was in vain. The words came out strained. Or maybe just honest. Come to think of it, that's what I'd been the entire night. Just honest with Hank.

He searched my face, a grin curving his lips upward. "No. You still look like a cowboy's dream come true."

My heart stumbled in my chest. "You're a romantic, Hank."

"Can't blame me. Not when I got a pretty girl here beside me."

A blush crept over my cheeks, and inside I swooned. "Is it true?" I nodded at his brown Stetson. "Wear the hat, ride the cowboy?"

He sat back, brow arched. "You want to find out?"

I let out a shaky breath. "Quite a line."

"No line." Gaze heated, he spun his empty whiskey glass on the table. "I want you to come back to my cabin."

Despite my sweaty palms, boldness took over, and I ran a hand up his arm. "A cabin in the woods. Sounds ominous."

He leaned in, lightly grazing a thumb across the arc of my cheekbone. "Ominous ain't the word I'd use to describe what I plan to do with you, sugar."

Awareness, desire curled that vibrating thread between us.

My core tightened, but I played it cool, arching a brow. "You take a lot of girls back to your cabin, cowboy?"

A serious expression overtook his rugged face. "Just the ones I want."

My heart fluttered. My toes curled. In those six seconds of flirty bar banter, I already knew I loved a cowboy.

"Bell."

I blink away the memory of being pinned against the wall of this very cabin that night. Of the moment he dropped to his knees and slid off my jeans to press a hot kiss to the inside of my thigh.

"What?" My voice comes out breathless.

As my mind clears, I take in the cabin again, discovering it's darker than it was when we entered.

"We got a problem." His shoulders lift with his heavy sigh.

"What is it?" I force my legs to move and drift to the window where he's standing.

"That."

I follow his finger to the sky. "Shit."

3

Hank

Leave it to the sky to unleash while I'm arguing with Bellamy. Freezing rain spirals from the bleak gray sky, and there are already at least two inches of snow on the ground.

"What does this mean?" Bellamy presses her palms and the tip of her nose against the window like she's waiting for Santa Claus.

"It means it's a blizzard."

Nostrils flaring, she looks over her shoulder at me. That flash of fire in her amber eyes tells me she's pissed, and she makes a little shooing motion with her hands. "If you go now, you can make it home."

A scoff rumbles low in my chest. "Great idea. Why not take a leisurely drive in a superstorm that can down power lines and strand me in my car for an extended period of time?"

The wind howls, the cabin creaking as if to illuminate my point. Last year's storm wreaked havoc on Silverwood, turning Main Street into an icy ghost town.

I huff a laugh. "Or maybe you'd like that, Bell."

"No. I wouldn't like that." She raises her chin. Exhales stoically. "So. Again. What does this mean?"

I shrug. "I guess this means we're stuck together."

Her calm façade cracks. She tosses her hands up. "Great. This is just fucking great."

I study my ex-wife. Tiny and messy haired and ferocious. Like some beautiful forest creature emerging from her winter hollow to rip me a new one.

And yet. My heart misses a beat, and then another. *Still so goddamn beautiful.*

Her dark chestnut hair's longer than it was when I last saw her, wild and unbound like she can't be bothered to brush it. Creamy white skin. Sharp collarbones. A straight nose, freckles dancing over the bridge. Her burgundy lipstick makes her amber eyes pop.

I tear a hand through my hair. Dammit. I hate the reaction my body still has to her. "Relax. It'll be cleared up in a day or two."

"That's still too long." Her mouth purses into a thin line that makes me think she'd rather shack up with the corpse of Charles Manson than be trapped here with me.

Bitterness gathers in my chest.

I pinch the bridge of my nose, breathing through a growl. "Trust me, Bluebell, I don't want to be here anymore than you want me here."

She glares at me. "Don't call me that."

Fuck. Why, three years later, is her sweet nickname still stuck on the tip of my tongue?

"Bellamy Blue," I whispered on our wedding night. "That name was made for you, sugar."

"I was made for you." She rolled over, into my arms, kissed the hollow of my throat.

"Bluebell. My bluebell."

Gripping her thighs, I made my way down her body. When I came to the heat, the heart of her, I breathed her in. Pressed my mouth against her slickness and licked and bit and teased. I was famine and she was a feast, and goddamn, I was ravenous.

Her whole body trembled. "Hank." Her hands went to my hair and hung on. All she could say was my name. But I knew what she meant.

I never wanted to taste anyone else, ever.

Bellamy shucks off her fur-trimmed parka, the rustling sound of it stealing my attention, and drapes it over the back of the leather couch.

I stiffen. Her tight white long-sleeved thermal hugs her full breasts. Those leggings do the same justice to her pert little ass. My cock jerks in my jeans.

Bellamy's always been beautiful, but I think her evil superpower is she keeps getting hotter. Sexier.

Thirty will look damn good on her.

Clearing my throat to conceal a groan, I turn away.

I'm a man. A cowboy. It's called motherfucking control, for Christ's sake.

One of the walkies blasts from its perch on the kitchen shelf.

Grateful for the distraction, I stomp across the room and grab it up. "Pops? You okay?"

As I turn and prop myself up against the counter, I catch the hint of a smile on Bellamy's face. She's always had a soft spot for my father. The feeling is mutual. Back when we were dating, he saw her sneaking out of my place one morning, offered to cook her breakfast and told her to call him if I ever so much as put a tear in her eye.

"Doin' just fine. You kids hangin' in up there?" My father chuckles, too much humor in his tone. "Or should I ask if you're still alive?"

I press the button on the side of the walkie and respond. "We're alive."

"For now," Bellamy mutters as she hangs up her jacket.

"Gonna close up the tree farm until this storm blows over. If we're lucky," he says, sorrow staining his voice, "we'll still get to open on Christmas Eve."

I close my eyes. I've been dreading this day all year.

"I'll take care of the horses." I clear the emotion from my throat. "I can get around on the snowmobile."

"Stay warm, son."

Eyes narrowed, Bellamy takes a single step closer. "What was all that about?"

"Nothin'." I head for the front door and rip it open. "I'm goin' to get firewood."

Without another word, I turn my back on Bellamy

and head into the flurry of snow and wind. The granite peaks west of us are barely visible by now. Fuck. If we get stuck without heat, we'll have a hell of a time. I brought a few logs in yesterday, but we'll need more if this storm continues, and they'll need time to dry. Working quickly, I gather as much wood as I can. Then I return to the cabin and stack it in the entryway.

By the time I'm finished and wiping snow from my shirtsleeves, Bellamy has removed her boots, and Zelda, traitor that she is, is curled up on the rug, watching her unpack her things. A familiar paint-stained backpack that I know contains easels and art supplies sits in a corner of the room.

The sight of it makes something in my chest wrench. *Fuck.*

She came up here to paint. She's got a whole new life now. Successful. Maybe a man. A boyfriend.

My heart gives a painful lurch. Fuck. I don't want to know. How she's moved on without me.

Bellamy plunks a duffel bag on the counter. Out come fancy meats. Cheeses. Nuts.

"What's that?"

"Girl dinner."

No wonder she's so thin.

Scoffing, I stride past her to the fridge. "That's not dinner. That's food for mice."

She rolls her eyes and pulls out a small jar of chocolate-covered almonds. "Well, I like mice dinner, then."

Beer in one hand, ground beef in the other, I spin around. "Good thing I stocked the place for Christmas."

"*My* Christmas," she shoots back, cheeks flushed, eyes bright.

"Yeah, well, you're welcome for not starving over the weekend." I take a long sip of my beer, then roll up my shirtsleeves and wash my hands. "You take the loft."

She arches a brow. "I planned on it." Her teeth sink into her lush lower lip as she bends to grab her overnight bag. "I'm going upstairs to unpack."

"Be careful." Even now, it's ingrained.

She stiffens, but rather than respond, she scurries to the ladder, in a hurry to get away from me.

Below her, Zelda whines, pawing at the first rung. While I brown ground beef, I keep one eye on Bellamy, making sure she doesn't fall.

This was a mistake. A bad fuckin' idea. But you're full of those, aren't you, Hank?

I couldn't resist coming back here. How could I, when my brain is still stuck on Bellamy?

At twenty-two, I knew a few things. I liked horses. A damn good rodeo. I'd work the ranch, eventually take over my father's Christmas tree farm. And I knew I'd know the one when I saw her. That night in Buck's Bar, Bellamy was it.

I knew I'd be taking her home that night. The perfectly smudged eyeliner, the bold way she approached me, the drawing. Fuck, I was a goner. We drank whiskey, popped quarters into the tiny jukebox and talked about life and Christmas trees.

When we woke the next morning and she said she had to go back to San Francisco, I said stay. She called in sick.

For the entire week.

We did long distance for six months before I asked her to marry me. I never expected her to sacrifice her dreams for me. She was only twenty. She had so much waiting for her in California. But that night, parked on that dusty back road lined with big trees and bathed in moonlight, I laid it all out.

"I'll move, Bell. I already told Pops—"

"No." She laughed like I was being ridiculous. "I want to stay here with you."

"Sugar—"

"I love Silverwood, and I love you." The ring on her finger glinted as she brought her small hand to my cheek. She gave me a flirty little smile. "So shut up, cowboy."

I kissed her then, hard, almost pleading. So damn in love with her I swore my heart would crack through my chest just to sync with hers.

Even now, it still eats at me. Guilt over letting her give it all up. But she loved the farm and the ranch, so who was I to argue? I felt so goddamn lucky. Like I had gotten everything I'd ever wanted in life.

By the time I crawl out of my thoughts and Bellamy returns, the fire is roaring and the sauce is nearly finished. She's changed into gray sweatpants and an oversized Christmas T-shirt that reads *I Do It For the Ho's*. She's washed her face. Tamed her dark hair into glossy waves.

She fiddles with the radio, settling on a Christmas station. She's still Bellamy. A hopeless Christmas romantic. Me, I lost that spirit when she walked away.

"Can we not?" It comes out gruffer than intended. "With the Christmas music?"

Her eyes widen in surprise. "You love Christmas music."

"Not today."

"Fine." Brow furrowed, she scans my face. Then she changes it to an old country station, one of my father's favorites.

Merle Haggard croons, his voice filling the old cabin.

Phone in hand, Bellamy steps closer, almost a shy tiptoe. "What are you making?" She rests a hip against the counter, peers over the island, wrinkles her nose.

I chuckle. "Like you can afford to be picky when you brought mice food."

She smiles. Barely. I may have spent the last three years without her, but even I can tell she's faking it. It doesn't reach her eyes.

It bothers the fuck out of me. I'm a fixer. That used to be my job. Help Bellamy. Make her laugh. Give her anything she damn well wanted.

Even if it wasn't me.

"Spaghetti." I flip off the burner. "Pasta's done."

She nods almost absentmindedly, then steps into the kitchen. Quietly, she uncorks a bottle of wine and pours herself a glass. Then she retrieves two plates from the cupboard where I've always kept them. I blink at the easy action. For an instant, it's like we traveled back in time, and it sends a pang of wistfulness through my chest.

Focusing on the task at hand, I back up to drain the pasta. She moves. But the kitchen's a small space and we find ourselves plastered together. She twists around, her chest sweeping against mine, her honey scent wafting over me. I get lost in her—her freckles, the caramel flecks in her eyes.

Fuck. I'm sweating through my shirt and my feelings thanks to that damn fire. Jesus. I'm still staring. Still 100 percent doomed.

What was I thinking coming up here?

I take a step back. "Shit. Sorry."

She does too. "No. My bad."

Our voices are formal, like we're locked in some strange dance we don't know the moves to.

It's fucking weird. To see her after three years, to be trapped together. How the hell are we going to co-exist until the blizzard blows over when I'm already falling apart?

And if I know her, she is too.

She flinched when she crossed the threshold. She thinks she's putting on a cool front, but she doesn't fool me. She's still not over it. Which makes two of us.

The day she left comes rushing back in my memory.

As soon as she stepped into the kitchen, I felt it. The air was too tense. Her eyes were wet with tears as she placed her ring in the fruit dish and said she wanted a divorce.

"What can I do, baby?" I pleaded. "Whatever it is, I'll fix it."

She laughed softly. "You can't fix this, Hank."

"I can. Bluebell, just let me try."

She gave me a sad smile and picked up a suitcase that looked way too light. "I just need some time. Okay?"

So, holding out hope that time would bring her back to me, I let her go. But she was stubborn and I was a fool, and what happened next was inevitable.

We dish in, each of us taking our plate. I sit at the table, but Bellamy perches at the kitchen island. The distance she keeps pisses me off. I stab at a mushroom.

How the fuck did we get here? We went through the worst thing two people could go through together. And instead of leaning on one another, we fell apart.

I'm not over her. Not by a long shot.

We didn't marry too young. Or fight all the damn time. Or cheat. We were happy.

Until we weren't.

Being around her again has stirred all those emotions up. But I can't tell her I miss her every second of every day. I can't admit that I daydream about her, that I still have to fight the urge to text *good morning* to her. Three years feels like three days. I can still hear her giggly laugh in the mornings, see that mess of dark hair moving under the covers.

"So."

I blink at the husky sound of her voice. Bellamy twirls a strand of pasta, deciding on a neutral subject. "The farm."

Fuck. That's the last topic I want to discuss.

I run a hand through my hair, lean back in my chair. "What about it?"

"How's it doing?" She shifts on the stool, one foot dangling, like she's ready to run. "Seemed busy when I got here."

"It's surviving. Just like all of us."

She makes a little sound of affirmation. "Where's your Bronco? I didn't see it in the yard."

I grimace, my chest pinching. "Sold it."

Her eyes are wide. "You loved that Bronco."

I did. A classic 1966 cherry-red Bronco. Restored by my own hands.

"Yeah," I sigh. "Well, things change."

Silence engulfs us as we look at each other. Even Zelda's staring.

"What about you?" I ask before she can pry further. She's pushed me, and it makes me want to push her. "You plan to paint while you're here?"

She won't. Bell's always been superstitious about her work. No one sees her paintings until the very end. Not even me.

"Luka thinks I should."

Goddamn if my shoulders don't get tight. It's what I thought. She's moved on.

"Luka?" I fight to keep a cool head even as jealousy slices deep. Even as I keep a death-grip on my fucking fork, wishing it were Luka's neck.

Is he the asshole who takes care of her now? I wasn't ready to give up the title of husband three years ago, and I still mourn its loss. The idea of someone else taking it over stings.

"My new agent," she says.

A loud breath escapes me.

Thank Christ.

"Anyway." She picks up her wineglass and drains it. "I haven't painted anything really worthwhile, since—" Face flushing, she cuts herself off.

"Since you left?" I can't stop from directing my annoyance, my anger at her.

With a sigh, she sets her fork down. "Don't."

"Why not?"

"It's too hard." She shakes her head, eyes fluttering closed. "I don't want to talk about it."

"That sounds about right. You not wanting to talk." A wave of melancholy sweeps over me.

"I know I left. But you left too. In your own way." Her voice is a hollow void of emptiness.

"Whatever you have to tell yourself to make it better."

"Fuck you, Hank." Fire flashing in her amber eyes, Bellamy pushes back from the island. Zelda leaps into action, pacing around the table, her anxious, insistent whines filling the kitchen.

"This was a stupid idea," Bellamy says, exhaling a dark little sob. "You staying here."

Guilt rolls through me. Dammit, I'm an asshole.

The tear that tracks down her cheek almost breaks my heart in half.

I reach for her. To fix this. To pull her into my arms and hold her. "Sugar—"

"Don't call me that." Then she's gone, climbing up the ladder to the loft without another word.

Whining, Zelda paws at my pant leg.

"Fuck." I drop my head into my hands.

4

Bellamy

DECEMBER 21ˢᵀ

HANK'S BED IS WARM AND SOFT.

Strike that.

My bed is warm and soft.

I shift, burying myself further into the blankets, listening to the howl of the wind outside, the scrape of the branches against the side of the A-frame.

Finally, with a sigh, I kick tangled blankets from my legs. I pad across the chilly floor and peer over the railing, surveying the living room and kitchen below.

Hank's gone.

For a moment, there's a twinge of regret in my lungs,

but I push out a breath. Good. After last night, we need the space.

No doubt, despite the weather, he's out on the ranch, tending to the horses, helping Papa Blue. Quickly, I wash my face and change into jeans, a thick cable-knit sweater and fuzzy blue socks. I make the bed, pausing when I catch sight of the photo of Zelda wearing a wreath around her neck, then climb the ladder.

Downstairs, I find a full coffeepot, the red light telling me it's still hot. I pour myself a cup and bring it to my nose, inhaling its hazelnut scent. Absentmindedly, I stare out the window where a dizzying swirl of snowflakes falls from the slate sky.

Hank's still pissed I left.

I don't know how to tell him that I had to.

I swallow, blinking back tears as the rabbit hole of memories sneaks up on me. My hand drifts, down, down, down to my stomach.

It's been three years since I lost Cody, and I still haven't gotten over it.

Losing a baby at twenty-two weeks. It wasn't supposed to happen. The second trimester is supposed to be safe. Happy.

The doctors said it was a placental abruption. That it could have killed me along with our baby. That I should consider myself lucky. But I didn't feel lucky. It felt like a crushing weight on my chest, in my heart.

Hank tried so hard to be strong, but he was just as devastated as I was. We'd been married for six years, but that day, in the hospital, was the first time I'd ever seen my husband cry.

After we came home from the hospital, I didn't want to talk about it. It was all Hank wanted to do. When I wouldn't talk, he went to Buck's.

I loved being pregnant. I was so happy to give Hank a baby. To start our family. Then, in one moment, our little dream was gone. I was devastated. I couldn't be around it. Couldn't be around Hank. Couldn't stand the sadness, the brokenness in those beautiful eyes.

Everything hurt. Hank hurt. Our families hurt. Guilt consumed me. What-ifs took over my thoughts and I couldn't stop tearing myself apart. What if it was my fault? What if that little slip off the ladder was what had caused me to lose Cody? What if I'd gone for an extra checkup after it happened?

The doctors swore I did everything right, but I couldn't stop feeling like I should have protected my baby. Like I failed.

I was so scared, and I was certain I never wanted to try again.

"I don't want to have another baby." I gasped the words out after the doctor left my hospital room. Left me sewn up and sore and without my baby. My heart said it wasn't a time for rash decisions, but my brain had other ideas.

Hank, sitting beside my hospital bed, tightened his grip on my hand. "It's okay."

"Do you?"

"Bell." His ragged voice was a hook, tearing out my soul.

"Hank. Do you?"

"Not if it means losing you." His throat worked. Tears glittered in his sapphire eyes. *"I almost lost you once. I can't do it again."*

I didn't believe him. Hank should be a dad. He dreamed of it, and he'd be the best at it. I might have been terrified of having another baby, but that didn't mean Hank should be denied the chance. Why should I stop his life just because I couldn't give him what he deserved?

I thought leaving it all behind would help, would heal. But it hasn't. I've tried to fix the grief inside me. Tried to paint my way through it. Tried to ignore it. Tried to talk to a therapist. But nothing worked. Not fully. Everything inside me has felt shaken up but contained for so long. A soda can under pressure.

That little baby changed everything. Broke me. Broke us.

But only because I let it.

My stomach rumbles, snapping me out of my trance. Slowly, I wander to the fridge. Tilting my head, I take in its contents, then blink. Every shelf is full. A true Christmas feast. Pumpkin pie. Ham. Potatoes. Even the tin can of cranberry sauce I love and a random pack of candles stacked on top of a jar of mayo.

When I notice Papa Blue's infamous chocolate chip zucchini loaf, my mouth waters. Without a second thought, I grab it and carve myself a hunk. Then, like the heathen I am, I stand over the kitchen sink and inhale a giant slice.

As I chew, I take in the open space of the cabin.

In every crevice, a memory.

The archway where we'd meet under the mistletoe after

working a long day at the tree farm. "Kiss me," I'd say, pressing up on tiptoes to meet Hank's grinning mouth.

The fireplace where we'd hang stockings and then trade our ornaments. Every year, we'd get each other an ornament that best symbolized the year. The year we were married, I got Hank a cowboy and cowgirl couple, complete with matching boots and hats. Our fifth, the year I landed an agent, he got me an artist's palette.

Our last Christmas together, I put our sonogram in a mini rectangle ornament frame.

"Nugget." Hank got down on his knees in front of me on Christmas Eve. His voice was low and rough with joy. "That's it."

I sighed happily. "His name's not nugget."

Hank's hands flexed, then spread out on my belly. He laughed, glancing up at me. "Nickname, then."

"Yeah, sure, okay. But he needs a cowboy name," I added a bit more seriously.

"Whatever you want, Bluebell." He smiled up at me, unconcerned, big palms still on my belly, rugged yet gentle.

"Westley?"

By the twist of his lips, I could tell he hated it. But he'd never say it, so I went on.

"Cody?"

"Hmm. Like that one." He pressed a kiss on my belly.

"Me too," I said breathlessly.

Wrapping an arm around my waist, he pulled me closer. He inhaled. Exhaled. Breathed us both in.

I reached down, palming his smooth cheek. Feeling like there was something so big between us, something so, so special.

He looked up, like he already knew what I wanted to say.

"I love you too, sugar."

The memory washes over me like acid. "Fuck," I mutter, puffing a lock of hair out of my eyes and turning back to the sink.

I hate this.

I shouldn't be here.

Stuck in a cabin for God knows how long with my ex-husband? It's my worst nightmare. I wasn't counting on Hank being here. He makes it worse. The memories. I wanted to deal with my demons alone.

I need to keep myself busy.

Sighing, I scan the room. The fireplace, the bookshelf and chairs. The corner where we always put our tree.

Bare. This place is so damn bare. There's nothing, not even a scrap of Christmas cheer.

That's what I'll do.

I'll decorate.

It's exactly what I need. Mindless work to take my mind off everything. The memories. Hank's surly attitude. The storm roaring outside.

To set the mood, I make a fire. Then, from the small storage space, I pull out two boxes and a large plastic tote.

I open the first box and laugh. I can't help it. Hank's décor is ridiculous. He's cheesy like that. He loves fruit cake and the not-so-politically-correct 1964 *Rudolph the Red-Nosed Reindeer* movie. While he preferred traditional Christmas décor—gaudy red and green decorations and multicolored lights—I preferred a more minimalist approach. Bare garland, creamy ivory stockings and white lights that screamed winter wonderland.

Our different tastes made us bicker and laugh and tease, but we made it work. We always made it work.

Until we couldn't.

I lift a one-eyed nutcracker. Then dump it back in the box.

Nope. This is my Christmas.

For the next few hours, I busy myself with unpacking. By the time noon rolls around, I've successfully sorted the decorations and the snow globes, and I've untangled the lights.

That's when I realize Hank's décor and mine have been mixed together so thoroughly, they've merged into one gigantic pile.

I swallow.

It never used to be like this.

It's so sad that we're now living two completely separate lives, when for so long, they were one. We were one. Loved careful and close. Like a secret between two souls.

For some, Christmas means big, chaotic families, early mornings and a hundred activities, but for Hank and me, it meant our cabin. It meant five days of cozy cooped-up togetherness. Late mornings tangled in the sheets, then working the tree farm with Papa Blue in the afternoons. At night, we lit a fire and decorated for the upcoming holiday.

Dropping into a crouch, I dig through a box and feel the soft edge of fabric, a small loop catching my index finger. I pull out the decoration, along with the second just like it, and hold them up in front of me. Our stockings.

I bite my lip. Do I hang Hank's? Why would I? He's not staying.

I agonize over the decision, my chest aching, then decide to hang neither. Back in the box they go.

I'm chewing on a candy cane and pondering next decorating steps when the door flies open. The blast of air rustles the garland wrapped around my neck like a boa.

Hank's cheekbones and the tip of his nose are bright pink, windswept. Snow dusts his Stetson, those broad shoulders covered in a thick Carhartt jacket. Zelda beelines for me, pawing my leggings and letting out happy yips as I rough her fur.

Maybe he means to, maybe he doesn't, but he stops at the threshold.

My mind instantly goes to our tradition. Of meeting there after work. How he leaned in. How warm his mouth was against mine, his big hand sliding up my cold throat and cradling my jaw as he kissed me.

The memory is quickly sideswiped by another.

Blood. Footprints.

If I could burn this memory, I would.

Hank's mouth moves. He's speaking, but I've heard none of it.

I shake my head. "Sorry, what?"

Zelda barks, weaving her way around my legs, like *snap out of it, Mom.*

His eyes follow mine, up to that star-shaped hook. Then he quickly moves deeper into the cabin and shuts the door.

"How are the animals?" Bent at the waist, I scratch Zelda behind her cold ears.

"Pissed. Hungry. But alive." He's business as usual as he shrugs off his jacket, revealing a thick thermal shirt. He shakes off the snow, then hangs his jacket on a hook. Looks at me with a furrowed brow. "What are you doing?"

"I'm decorating." I crunch the end of the candy cane.

"You ain't serious." He rubs his palm across his sharp jaw and peers over my head, sapphire eyes scanning the snow globes scattered across the fireplace mantel.

I tilt my chin at the unhappiness in his voice. "Has anyone ever told you, you lack Christmas spirit?"

"Just the ghost of my past." He takes off his Stetson and drops it on the entry table.

"What's with you?" How is it possible that he suddenly dislikes Christmas? First the music, now the decorations. "You've always been a sucker for a good nativity scene. And now you're acting like you've been possessed by the Grinch."

"Yeah, well, first time for everything."

"Deal with it. I'm decorating." I give a little shrug. "Especially because you stole my Christmas."

Hank emits a derisive snort. "Stole's a little dramatic, ain't it, Bluebell?"

With a roll of my eyes, I twist, twirling the piece of garland off my shoulders. I press up on tiptoes and weave the faux pine strands between the snow globes.

"That'll burn." Hank's deep voice carries. The floorboards vibrate beneath his boots as he moves closer, crowds my space.

"No, it won't." I pull away from him and peer up at his handsome face, at the deep and serious frown. Whiskers shadow his jaw, his skin still tan from the summer sun. "It never has before."

"I'm tellin' you, Bell, it will." Sighing, he reaches around me and tugs the garland down. Then he tosses it onto the leather couch. "You got the fire goin' too hard. Last thing I need is to worry about you and the cabin burnin' down."

As he crouches and fusses with the logs, I back away, arms crossed, frustrated and wishing I was alone.

I'm supposed to be channeling my inner Monet while I'm here. I'm supposed to be having girl dinner and crying into my wine. Nursing hot cocoa and watching rom-coms. Not fighting with my ex while simultaneously fighting the urge to count each and every snowflake in that whiskery scruff of his.

"You don't have to worry about me," I mutter.

He stands, the big, stiff line of his body twisting toward me.

"I always worry about you." The words are a heated huff as he storms into the kitchen.

My stomach flips over. I don't know what to make of that statement. I just know I like it. Too much.

Hands propped on my hips, I study him, befuddled by the man. The only thing more frigid than the Montana air? Hank Blue's cold shoulder.

'Tis the season for a grumpy cowboy, apparently.

"There's still coffee," I offer kindly. But only because I want something from him.

He pours himself a cup, then chops a hunk of zucchini

bread. All the while, the wind continues to gust outside, making the cabin vibrate and groan. He eats the sweet treat with a lifted brow, his smug gaze on me, but says nothing.

I blush at having been caught eating his food.

He swallows, then sighs, long and loud. "What do you want, Bell?"

I tug at a lock of hair. Am I really that obvious? "I need help."

"With what?"

"Getting the ornaments from the shelf."

"One problem with that. We don't have a tree." Frustration tightens his features.

"So let's get one."

He stares at me and I stare back, the silence heavy. The tension? Radioactive.

"I want a tree, Hank," I say, staring wistfully at the corner where it should go.

Once again, I'm hit with that stern cowboy frown. The one he used to give the horses when they escaped their pens. Dusting his hands of crumbs, he eases closer. He doesn't stop until he's standing in front of me. "You're not getting a fucking tree, Bell."

"Please?" I push my lower lip out into a well-practiced pout, one he could never say no to.

His face falls, but he regroups quickly.

Hank Blue's always been a stubborn cowboy.

"That's not fair," he growls, leaning in. Every atom in my body tenses, simmering with heat. "You don't get to do that anymore. Pout."

"Fine." I turn my back to him, storm for the door and pluck my jacket from its hook. "I'll get one myself."

Papa Blue and Hank taught me the correct way to cut down a Christmas tree. I can do it on my own. No man needed.

He follows me, his long legs eating up the distance between us. When one of his big hands palms my hip, spinning me around to face him, my breath rushes out of me. "Bell, there's a fucking blizzard outside. You're not going out there."

"The snow's stopped."

"Do you see the clouds?" he fires back. "If we're lucky, we have an hour before the storm ramps up again."

Of course I saw the clouds. But at this moment, I don't care. All I want is a tree. All I want is for Hank to stop being so stubborn. Why does he suddenly hate Christmas?

Why do I fucking care?

I inhale deeply, wishing I could forget it. But I can't. I have to know. "I don't understand," I say, my voice more pleading than I'd like. "You've always loved Christmas."

"Not anymore."

"But why?" I'm horrified when tears fill my eyes. But when he looks at the toes of his boots rather than responding, I persist. "But why, Hank? Why—"

"Why?" Voice raw, nearly feral, he catches my wrist and pulls me toward him. "Christ. Because of you, Bellamy."

At that tiny touch, sparks, so many sparks, crackle between us. Hank's everywhere. Haunting the past, my heart. Hands on my thighs, his lush mouth sweeping over my throat, gravelly morning voice.

"You don't mean that." I flatten my hand on his broad chest and push him hard enough to separate us.

"I do mean that." He steps forward, his eyes sharp as steel. "Because it hasn't been the same since you left." His chest heaves. "Nothing has been the goddamn same since you left."

My insides twist into a hundred knots of confusion, of desire.

I search for a response, a reassurance. Because Hank without his Christmas spirit is like hot cocoa without marshmallows, but all that comes out of my mouth is a pathetic, whimpered noise.

His laugh is angry now. "So if you're askin' why I'm actin' like an asshole, like some fuckin' scrooge, it's plain and simple. I hate Christmas."

"You don't mean that." I clutch my hands to my heart. He might as well take a knife and gut me.

"I do." His jaw ticks. "Fuck Christmas."

I gasp, stagger back a step. "Take it back."

"I have more work to do," he grits out. Almost like he's talking to himself rather than me. "I don't know why I'm fuckin' here anyway."

"Then go." Tears burn my eyes. Heart pounding in my ears, I edge backward. "You never stayed when things got hard anyway."

A ragged breath escapes him, his face paling, his expression so pained that it steals the air from my lungs.

It was a low blow. A lie. If I could take it back, I would.

But he doesn't give me the chance.

He snatches his Stetson and storms out, slamming the door behind him.

I curl my fingers into fists, feel the sharpness of my fingernails as they make moons in the heel of my palm.

I'm getting a damn tree if it's the last thing I do.

5

Hank

FUCK CHRISTMAS.

My words echo in my head, heartless, thoughtless, as I slam into my workshop behind the cabin.

It was an asshole thing to say. Bellamy looked like I had just told her I strangled a litter of kittens.

I didn't mean it. I blame my bad temper on the debt we're trying to get out from under.

In four days, we lose everything.

I start up the wood-burning stove, eyeing the slightly open door every few seconds, waiting for Zelda. She doesn't show. Fucking perfect. My goddamn dog would rather be with Bellamy.

Tension tightens my neck. I roll out my shoulders, huffing in frustration, my breath a white cloud. I wish I'd grabbed my jacket, but I'd rather freeze to death than go back for it. I need some goddamn time away from Bellamy. Away from what she's doing to me.

I want her. So goddamn bad it hurts.

I've spent so long thinking about taking this chance, and now that I have, now that I'm here, I feel like an idiot.

What the hell was I thinking coming here? I knew it was her weekend, and foolishly, I came anyway. And for what? Some harebrained notion that I could get her to stay? That I could tell her I miss her, I love her, I can't live without her?

Instead, all we've done is bark and bite at each other.

My fault. I brought up the past, took my anger out on her. Hell, I told her I hate Christmas, even after I brought along all her favorite Christmas dishes.

I don't hate Christmas.

I just miss her.

Miss her in a way that's feral and greedy and damn near makes me insane. Knowing she's on my ranch, back in our Christmas cabin, is torture. She's here but she's not mine. She's close but I can't touch her.

How many dreams have I woken from still tasting that perfect pussy, those breasts? With that giggly laugh echoing in my head? Those small hands running up my chest, her candy-apple-red mouth parting to say, "I love you, Hank."

With a pained grunt, I shake my head, trying my damnedest to dislodge the memories.

Needing a task to keep me busy, I heft an old saddle

from the rack and settle at the workbench. I get out a needle and thread and begin to stitch up a tear near the front of the seat.

I haven't been the same since she left.

I could have rallied. Could have gotten my life together, seen my friends, moved on. Instead, I pulled away, shut down. I couldn't forget her.

Because Bellamy Blue is still mine.

I stick myself with the needle, my hands too unsteady, and curse. Exhaling, I lift my head and focus on the painting hanging over my workbench.

One of Bellamy's.

The gold leaf and silver flecks she used make it shine. Violent slashes of blues and greens and red streak across the canvas. But in those messy layers of paint, a lilac sunset slowly fading to gold, is a house. A ranch. She painted our cabin.

That first year after we were divorced, I flew to San Francisco, praying she'd hear me out. Praying she'd come home. It was the night of her big art show. I crossed the showroom floor, her ring in my pocket. But when I saw her, smiling bright and beaming, I stopped in my tracks.

I couldn't do it. Not when she looked so damn happy.

I left without seeing her. Before she knew I was there.

But I had to have some part of her, so I bought her painting.

How different would my life be if I had just talked to her that day? I'll never know. But I could have walked across that showroom floor and kissed her. Should have. Should have told her how proud I was of her. Spilled my guts and told her I wanted her back. That I was a fucking idiot who didn't deserve her, but that I wanted to try again.

But I didn't.

Just because I couldn't live without her doesn't mean she felt the same way.

The door cracks open slowly, and my heart stumbles. Breath held, I look over, hopeful it's Bellamy. But it's my dad, shuffling inside, flecks of snow blending with his white hair.

"Pops." I sigh. "You shouldn't be out in this weather."

"I'm an old man, son." He tips his hat at me as he settles into a chair next to the stove. "If I go out like Frosty the Snowman, so be it."

"Jesus." I set down the needle and thread. "You're a morbid bastard, you know that?"

"Tell me somethin', Hank." He steeples his fingers in front of his face, a familiar gesture that tells me I'm in for a lecture. "You're out here, Bellamy's in there."

I grimace at the reminder.

"You tell her about the farm yet?"

"Do I need to?"

His eyes narrow, seeing right through me. "She deserves to know."

The silence lingers between us. My father looks older, more tired than he did a few months ago, and for damn good reason.

We're in the shitter with the bank. The tree farm and the surrounding land, including the cabin, are scheduled to go to auction the week after Christmas. The only way to keep that from happening is to come up with back taxes.

Thinking about Bellamy inside the cabin, *our* cabin, makes me want to save it that much more.

But I don't know how.

"She doesn't deserve to know," I mumble, looking away from him. "We're divorced."

My father's bushy brows draw together. "Hell, I thought you came up here to keep her. To win her back."

"I thought I could, but…" Bell's words from last night come back to me. "It's too hard," I say quietly.

My dad looks at me like he did the time he found me smoking a cigarette and made me smoke the whole pack. "Kid, you've never been a quitter. Not when your mama died. Not when that roan got stuck in the river with a broken ankle. Not when you met that girl and made it work, even though she lived a thousand miles away."

The ache in my chest flares. "Yeah, well, I'm quittin' now." I shove up from the workbench and pace, needing to move. "She doesn't want me back, Pops. She's made that pretty damn clear."

"Then stop pining and get out there and date."

I pull up short and give my father a sharp look. The smile twitching his lips tells me he knows what he's doing. His words are a dare. One I'll never take him up on.

I've been on a few miserable blind dates. I've gone out, looking for a girl to pick up. But the truth is, I haven't been with a woman in three damn years.

Sure, I'm horny as hell, but not for just anyone. For Bellamy. My wife. We may have signed papers, but she's still mine. My wife. My girl. My bluebell.

I love her so damn much.

Never stopped. Never will.

From the moment I saw her in that bar, I considered her mine. The way she approached me, ballsy yet shy, bowled me over. That feeling only grew as the night went on, as we connected over music, the deaths of our parents. Over our love of Christmas. Her beautiful drawing, so hesitant, held so much hope. Just like her. My best friend, Clint, teased me for dating a city girl. I'd just grin and tell him she wouldn't be one for long.

Swallowing hard, I look down, flexing my hand. Watch my wedding band catch the remaining light filtering in through the windows.

My father clears his throat and peers at me from beneath the brim of his Stetson. "Christmas is a time for miracles."

"I don't believe in miracles." The memory of that day hits me. The opposite of a miracle. Pain and despair always choose the perfect fucking time to sneak up on me.

Coming home from the ranch to meet Bellamy beneath the mistletoe. Only, I didn't find Bellamy. I found bloody footprints instead. Heart in my throat, I followed them, racing through the cabin until I found my wife curled up on the bathroom floor.

Tears streamed down her pale face. She clutched her stomach with one hand. The other gripped her phone. "Hank," she gasped. "It hurts."

I didn't want to waste a second waiting for the paramedics, so I scooped her up and hauled ass to the hospital.

But it was too late.

We lost Cody.

We lost our son.

The worst fucking time in my life.

I'd never felt so powerless.

Eyes closed, I rub at the sting in my chest.

"You lost a baby. Hell, you nearly lost your wife. That pain will never go away." My father's voice is stern, but when I force myself to look at him, his craggy face is sympathetic. "You're mad at the world, son. Mad at everyone. Bell left, but—"

"She left because I wasn't there for her."

After we lost our son, I made work my priority. I stayed out all day on the ranch, putting myself into backbreaking tasks that helped me forget, if only for a little while. I couldn't fucking bear to look at the room Bellamy had painted a cheery sunshine yellow. Her quiet sobbing in bed gutted me. I'd hover, not knowing how to help her. The weight was crushing. I had to be strong, calm. I had to hold it all together even as she pushed me away. And when she did, I went to Buck's Bar and drank in silence until my father arrived with words of common sense and threats to put a boot up my ass.

He grabbed me by the front of the shirt and tossed me against the side of my Bronco. "Get your shit together, son."

"Fuck this entire world," I blasted, the parking lot and my father blurring in front of me thanks to the whiskey. "Fuck everything."

"I don't disagree, kid. But right now, there's someone else hurting more than you."

"Bellamy." Just her name had the power to make me cave

in on myself. I dropped my head into my hands and cursed my stupidity.

"You can't heal her. She doesn't want to be healed."

I lifted my face, wiped at my eyes. "So what do I do?"

"You sober up. You go and love her. Just be there."

I did that. I stopped going to Buck's. I tried like hell to talk to her. But she shut down.

Six months later, she left her ring on the kitchen counter and walked out.

Our divorce was my fault. The biggest failure of my fucking life. She needed my help to move on, and I failed.

"But you're here now," my father says gently. "She's got some pain. You both do. Christmas seems like a mighty fine time to work out the kinks."

"Kinks." A ragged scoff pops out of my mouth. "We're fucking divorced, Pops."

"And it's a damn shame." He rises and heads for the door. With his hand on the knob, he pauses and eyes me over his shoulder. "We'll be okay without the farm. But will you be okay without her?"

I don't respond. He and I both already know the answer.

No. Without Bellamy, I won't be okay.

I look at her painting again. The swoopy lines and pretty colors. It's our cabin. Whether she wants to admit it or not. Even a year after leaving me, she painted us.

No cowboy in his right mind would be this fucking stupid.

I won't let her go. Not again.

6

Bellamy

'TIS THE SEASON FOR BAD IDEAS.

I trudge deeper into the glimmering forest, my boots slurping through knee-high snow, keeping the A-frame of the cabin in my sight so I don't get turned around. The last thing I need is to get lost or eaten by a coyote.

Though Hank would probably enjoy that.

Beside me, Zelda bounces happily, her spotted fur dotted with fluffy white flakes.

I look up, blinking at the clouds. I better move fast. I have what I need to pick the perfect tree. On the sled Pops set me up with yesterday lay gloves, a saw, rope and a tarp.

I don't need Hank Blue's permission to venture out. We're divorced. So there.

I ease the sled around a low stump and push through a grove of too-perfect trees. I should stop here, cut one close to the house, but I don't want the perfect Hallmark Christmas tree. I prefer the weird ones. The unloved and unchosen. Trees with character and charm.

So I plod on.

The gray sky above suits my mood as I stew over our argument.

It doesn't make sense. If Hank hates Christmas so much, why is he here? Why did he bring enough food to feed an army of elves? Maybe he wanted that memory. Maybe he's like me.

Reliving that pain feels almost welcome. Familiar at least.

I hate the way he got to me. Warming my stomach and that spot between my legs. I hate what I said to him. I want to apologize, take it back, beg him to forgive me.

He may have pulled away after I lost the baby, but he was there. Hovering. Trying to help. To talk. To fix.

Me?

I shut out the one person who was there for me.

Not because our marriage couldn't be saved or because I was unhappy. I didn't stop loving Hank. I did it because it hurt. Everything hurt. And the only way I knew how to cope was to push.

Guilt sinks deep in my gut as I force myself to face the truth.

I thought that by leaving, I'd get over him. Get over us.

But I was fooling myself. Every Christmas—every day on this earth—spent without Hank has been blue.

Friends, my mother, my therapist told me that if I was patient, eventually, I'd wake up and find that I had moved on. That our past, the idea of us, would be a blip on the radar of my life. They were wrong.

Because I didn't walk away not loving Hank—I left knowing I still did.

It's why I stayed away. Avoided seeing him. Refrained from texting. Our spark never died, and that scared the hell out of me. No man had ever wound me up and turned me on like he did. My love for him hadn't faded, not one bit.

But I left anyway. To spare him more pain. To give him the space to get over a loss that was my fault.

It doesn't matter anymore anyway. We're divorced. I fucked us up. And now he wants nothing to do with me.

I sigh. I'm unwell and sad.

With a nervous laugh, I look at Zelda. "Mama's delusional, right?"

In answer, she barks twice and races ahead of me.

With each step I take deeper into the woods, the snow becomes thicker under my boots. Before long, I see it. A gnarled fluffy tree with a wide base. Perfectly whimsical and weird. Small enough for me to drag back to the house.

By the time I'm parking the sled near my chosen co-nifer, my fingertips are numb and my legs are exhausted.

I test a branch, making sure the tree's healthy and not too dry. After working the farm with Hank and Papa Blue for six years, I'm a pro at this.

As I finger the pine's needles, a memory comes. Our

third Christmas at Blue Mountain Farm. Hank and I sneaking off into the big red barn.

"Need you. Need you so goddamn bad, Bell." Snow clinging to his broad shoulders, he pressed me back against a stall, lips on my temple, the move nudging my wool hat over my eyes.

"Hank." I ripped my hands through his messy hair. We moved together frantically, hungrily. Like we weren't fucking every night in that cabin.

He clutched my hips, yanking me to him. When he tried to shove my thick pants down, I giggled. It was a chore with all those layers. He managed it, but only after an endless struggle of determined curses.

After entirely too long, he slid inside me. "Sugar." A pulse of warm breath. A whisper of my name.

I moaned, curling my hands over his hard biceps, and dropped my forehead to his, feeling just like that star topper on a Christmas tree. Glimmering, bright, the center of it all. Especially to Hank.

My blood thrummed. I wanted this cowboy forever. I'd never once felt like I'd thrown it all away. Like I'd given it all up for a man. It simply felt like I'd gotten everything I needed. Happiness. Love. Freedom.

He was mine. The Christmas tree farm was mine. And I loved them both with every bone in my body.

I shake my head, trying to clear it of Hank.

Damn that man. Maybe tonight, after I return victorious with my tree, I'll apologize. Maybe we can bond over my mice dinner. Doubtful, but I'll try.

If only I had done it three years ago.

Despite the regret that hits me hard and sharp, I square

my shoulders and lay my tools on the ground. Beside them, I position the tarp. When I've got it where I want it, I lie on top of it, then worm myself carefully under the tree. On my belly, I saw the stump close to the ground and straight across. I can worry about clearing the underbrush when I get it back to the cabin.

When the tree starts to lean, I quickly scoot out from under it, escaping to one side.

The wind picks up.

The butt of the evergreen kicks back. Suddenly, I'm moving backward too. I twist, watching in horror as the tree, acting like a sled, begins a downhill propulsion.

Adrenaline courses through my veins as I grasp for purchase, reaching for the small, brittle plants close by. I didn't see the steep hill on my walk, thanks to the snow. But now gravity is taking me—and my tree—down.

Panic clutches my throat as a dense slab of snow rushes past.

Shit.

Shit.

Shit.

And then I'm sliding.

Screaming.

Falling.

A warm wet nose on mine.

"Hank?" I murmur. If he wants to kiss me, all he needs to do is ask.

Slowly, I open my eyes. Zelda's snow-covered face hovers in front of me. "Hey, girl."

She whimpers, nudging at my arm.

I lift the limb, realization setting in. I'm not buried by the snow, but I'm trapped, nonetheless. Wedged deep in a snowbank with the tree on top of me and no room to wiggle, I feel like I've been run over by ten reindeer. The limbs of the fir scratch at my face, though, luckily, there's a small air pocket to my left that allows me to breathe.

Taking long, deep exhales, I will myself not to panic. It's a difficult feat with what feels like a million pounds sitting on my chest. I can't stretch. Can't even wiggle my toes. And it's cold. So very cold.

Ugh, God. I went down the hill like one of those cartoon animals stuck in a careening snowball. Luckily, my leather gloves and hat stayed put during my tumble. Though it's possible they'll just ensure a slower, more painful death.

Another whimper from Zelda pulls me out of my spiraling thoughts.

"I know. If I could move, I would." Grunting, I heave one shoulder, trying to free it. But it's useless. I'm stuck.

"Help!" I yell, but my voice is thin and weak in the silence of the wild.

Oh God. Hank will find me in the morning, wet and dead. I should have taken his advice and forgotten about the tree.

Hank.

I look into Zelda's eyes. She's the best chance I have. "Go get Daddy." At the word, she straightens up, her wagging tail barely visible through the branches between us. I make my voice forceful, stern. "Go, Zelda. Get help. Now, girl!"

She leaps, yipping once, then takes off into the snow.

My heart sinks as she disappears.

I'm an idiot. All this for a stupid tree.

Above me, the falling snow, whipped by the wind, obscures the sinking sun. Darkness is coming on quickly. Fuck. What a way to spend the night. I'll be buried here like Frosty the Snowman. No one will find me. I'll die alone in the freezing Montana wilderness.

I try again to wrench my shoulders free, causing the pine branches to scrape across my face. But the tightly packed snow grips my body, holding me in place in a frozen little coffin.

Tears blur my eyes. Cold seeps through my jacket. I shiver from head to toe, teeth chattering, bone-deep cold.

My arms, my eyelids are heavy. I yawn. *A nap,* I think. *Just five minutes.*

Hank's voice. *Don't go to sleep, Bellamy. Don't you dare.*

I dare.

7

Hank

THE CABIN'S EMPTY. I KNOW IT THE SECOND I STEP inside. Even so, I spend three minutes scouring the eight-hundred-square-foot space.

"Bellamy!" I call out.

Dread pools in my stomach as I turn to the window. The winter nights in Montana are long, daylight nearly gone. The wind whips, the blowing snow blurring out the world around the cabin.

Heart in my throat, I zero in on the front door. "She wouldn't," I lie to myself.

She would.

This is the girl who raised a passel of orphaned

opossums, sleeping in the barn next to them for weeks. The girl who gave up her job in San Francisco for a poor cowboy. There's no stopping her when her mind's set.

It's one of the things I love most about her. Yet it scares the hell out of me.

Worry roars, truck-like, through my blood. I rub a hand over my jaw, feel it tick. "Goddamn it, Bell."

She was upset and angry when I left this afternoon, but the very least she could have done is left a note.

A scratching sound makes my ears prick. I hold my breath, listening for the source. When I hear it again, I storm to the door and yank it open.

Zelda, covered in snow, shoots past me, barking and yipping, leaving a trail of wet, skittery paw prints on the hardwood floor.

She whines, the sound insistent, panicked. The sinking feeling in my stomach plunges to my boots.

If Zelda was outside, she must have been with Bellamy. If Zelda's back, and Bellamy's not…

Fuck.

Terror grips me, the pressure in my chest so tight I can't breathe.

I grab Zelda's collar and tug her to me, crouching. "Show me where she is, girl."

Zelda barks once, then, tail wagging, she yanks free of my hold and blasts through the open door.

With trembling hands, I pull on my jacket and gloves. Then I race out onto the front porch and into the snow.

She doesn't stop. She's already so far ahead. I hop on the snowmobile and gun it, catching up quickly.

The wind whips through the trees. Cold air bites at my skin. The air's white, obscuring my vision. As angry as I am, I'm worried. Scared shitless. This wouldn't have happened if I had helped her get a goddamn tree.

Now she's what? Lost in the fucking forest in the dead of winter?

Christ.

I race through the trees, branches snagging at my clothes. With each minute that passes, more snow accumulates. Fear trickles into my gut. My thoughts run wild with regret.

Is she warm enough? Is she still pissed at me? I hope she's pissed. Hope she went for a walk. Hope she's wandering up to the cabin now, victorious with her tree. When I see her, I'll gladly let her slap the ever-lovin' shit out of me.

I race blindly through the wind and the snow, searching for Bellamy. I won't stop until I find her.

I shouldn't have left her. I should have stayed. Fought through it and fought it out.

The whirlwind of grim thoughts silences when Zelda leaps over a snow-covered log and plummets down the side of the steep cliff.

"No!" I shout.

But I go right after her. The snowmobile takes a sharp nosedive, but I lock the track with the brake and ride it down straight.

I stop the snowmobile on a flat spot of packed snow and scan the area. Nearby, evidence of a partial avalanche, the rapid flow of snow down the hillside. A cluster of trees lay on their sides.

Not just trees.

Bellamy.

My heartbeat ceases to exist.

I leap off the snowmobile and race for Zelda. She's digging beside one of the fir trees, her movements frantic. On my knees beside her, I shove at the evergreen. Through the branches and bristles, a tuft of dark hair and the fuzzy pom of a hat. Terror holds me in its grip.

Please let her be okay. Please.

"Bellamy!" I shout. Adrenaline surges through my veins, my pulse roaring in my ears.

Ignoring the pain, the cold, I push my hands through the prickly tree branches, shoving them enough to expose Bellamy.

The sight of her closed eyes catches me by the throat. "Bell." I cup her pale face. Fuck. She's freezing. "Talk to me, sugar. Wake up."

Her eyes flutter open. "Hank," she croaks. Her voice, soft, pained, is the only thing holding me together.

"Are you hurt, baby?" I scan what I can see of her.

"N-n-no, I'm just s-s-stuck." There's a scrape on her cheek. Her lips are blue, her teeth chattering relentlessly. "I tried to g-get a-a t-tree, but—"

"Don't worry about the tree." I tug her hat lower onto her head, protecting her ears. "I'm gonna get you out of there." Ducking, I get in her face, forcing her to focus on me. "Right now, okay?"

"Y-y-yes."

I hate to move her, especially if she has serious injuries, but I don't have much choice. She's been out here too long.

Carefully, I shove the tree off her completely.

Her chest rises and falls with labored breaths.

I loop my arms beneath hers. "Hang on to me." I haul her toward me, wrenching her free of the firm hold the crater of snow has on her.

Coughing and gasping, she clings to me. She's soaked to the fucking bone, the damp and cold from her clothes sinking through mine.

I give a whistle, trusting Zelda to follow, then cradle Bellamy in my arms. Holding her to my chest, I push through the snow toward the snowmobile. I want to check her over right here and now, but it's too cold. I have to be logical. It's the only thing getting me from A to B without losing it.

Get Bell back to the cabin. Get her warm. Keep her safe. Fall apart later.

Her dark head lolls against my chest as I race back to the cabin. Uncontrolled shivers rack her body. I can't tell if she's conscious. Her breaths are ragged, but at least she's breathing.

The snow falls harder. I break through the trees and come to a stop in front of the cabin.

Inside, I set her in a chair, lay her back, then get to work lighting the fire.

Once it's going, all my attention is on Bellamy. "You need to get warm." I pull her to her feet, unzip her thick parka and toss it unceremoniously on the floor. She shivers uncontrollably, her skin sickly pale.

"I'm-s-so-I'm sorry, H-H-Hank. I just wanted a tree."

Hands clutched to her chest, she lists to the side like she'll fall over any second.

I grasp her upper arms, keep her upright. "I don't care about a fuckin' tree."

I could have lost you, Bell. I could have lost everything that matters.

Her teeth chatter. "C-cold…"

"I know. Fuck, I know." Making a decision, I reach for her wet clothes, suctioned-cupped to her body. "I'm gonna get you naked, sugar," I warn.

She nods, eyes glazed. When her shirt lands with a plop on the floor, I go for her boots and pants. When she's stripped down to her panties and bra, I grab the thermal blanket from the back of the couch and drape it over her slender shoulders, yanking it closed. Still, she shakes.

I swear, enraged by the stubborn chill that won't leave her bones.

Fuck. Too cold. She's still too cold. She needs more warmth.

"You need body heat," I grit out.

Bellamy's eyes go wide. "Y-yours?"

"Yes."

Her weak nod is all the permission I need.

I strip down, adding my jeans and shirt to the pile on the floor. She stares at me, opens the blanket. I step into her, my fingertips pressing her shoulder blades, pressing her against me. Her skin's still cold, but I hitch a breath as her perfect body settles around mine.

"Hank," she whispers against my collarbone, her breath the only thing warm about her. Her slender body quakes as I mold mine to hers. The snowflakes in her hair melt against my skin. The swell of her breasts presses into my chest with every inhale.

I kiss her mess of chestnut hair. Inhale the scent of pine and crisp, clean snow. "You're okay, baby. You'll be okay."

"I need this." She snuggles closer.

I smooth my palm down her spine to rest at the small of her back.

Does she mean warmth or me? Either way, I won't bother arguing with her.

"You have me." I tuck her trembling body close.

She tilts her hips into mine, bringing us flush.

Christ. It's all innocent, all in the name of keeping her warm, keeping her alive, keeping my own damn heart from stopping, and yet my cock jerks.

Bellamy's hands spread over my bare stomach. A gentle, hesitant, searching touch that causes my muscles to tense. Then she's sighing, sighing, her face in my chest. She adjusts her legs, wriggling them around my thigh, her heat soaking into me, the wetness gathering there obvious.

Fuck.

Desire, lust, love rockets through me. But I keep my cock in check. I need her safe. Need her warm.

She could have died out there. I could have lost her forever.

Flashes of that day in the hospital come back to me, and my stomach takes a nosedive. Bellamy bleeding, the doctor's warning: I could lose them both. Hitting my knees in that waiting room, begging someone up there to hear me, to take me first. Pleading with them to not take my girl. I close my eyes, fighting down the panic in my throat, and focus on the present. On the woman in my arms. Bellamy. My bluebell.

Safe. Alive. Here.

"Bell." Her name's a ragged moan, falling from my mouth. My hands run up her cold arms.

She lifts her face, amber eyes watery beneath dark lashes.

Overcome, I lean in. I kiss the apples of her cheeks, the tip of her nose, her eyelashes. Anything that needs warmth, I'll give it.

"Hank."

It's all we have the strength to say. Her name. My name. An oath. A beckoning.

She presses up on tiptoes, moving closer. There's a shock of cold as her mouth meets my cheek, then warm, searing heat. The only thing hotter than the fire in the cabin is the fire between us.

I turn my head, our lips barely touching.

She pulls back a fraction. Looks at me like she can sense it. Everything I've been wanting to say all these years. Maybe she can.

A battle of wills blazes between us. I want to kiss her. But I don't.

My hands itch to part the blanket and explore every inch of her beautiful body. It's been three years since I've touched her, but it feels like a lifetime.

Instead, I pull her closer, my arms banded around her hips. Her heart thumps steadily against me as she warms. Her cheek pressed to my chest, resting over my heart. Her long lashes dark on the curve of her pale cheek. Eyes closed. She's exhausted.

I move, gently, carefully, and she doesn't protest.

We settle on the rug in front of the fire. I tuck her fiercely against my chest, keeping her cocooned in the blanket, the curve of her ass nestled against my already-aching dick. Her head falls back on my shoulder. Firelight dances across her pale face. She stares up at me with dark, sleepy eyes and a smile.

"We're on the ground."

"We are."

"I can't move, Hank." Her voice is rough and scratchy. A sexiness to it that I like.

I let out a shuddering exhale. "Good. That means you're warm."

"Thanks to you," she says, her bottom lip quivering.

I trace her cheek with my thumb, dragging it down to the hollow of her delicate throat. "You'll be okay, Bell."

She nods, closing her eyes.

For a long second, silence. Then she sighs out, "I like your scruff, cowboy."

"You do, huh?" I chuckle. There's not a day Bellamy doesn't surprise me.

"Yes," she confesses, burrowing deeper into my lap. "It's very handsome."

A smirk ghosts my lips. "Hell, sugar, remind me to never shave again."

"I can do that."

Wriggling, she inches an arm out of the blanket and

finds my hand. My heart hammers as she curls her slender fingers around mine.

"Thank you for coming for me," she murmurs. "For finding me."

I swallow the emotions that claw at my throat. "There's not a chance in hell I'd let you go again."

Bellamy *mmms*, a sweet, soft sound. She's nodding off, the slow rise and fall of her chest signaling sleep is near.

My heart clenches. God, do I love her.

Zelda, content that we're okay, circles her dog bed twice, then curls into a ball, head on her paws, eyes on us.

I look down at Bellamy's sleeping face. Her lips, rosy and parted, push out slow, rhythmic breaths. My heart rate slows, matching hers, following the steady, calming beat.

I should move. Get her dressed, tear myself away from her. But I don't. I can't. Not when she's tucked in my arms, fragile and soft.

So I allow myself this moment with her. Do what I should have done when we lost our baby.

I stay.

When I wake later, from a sleep so deep it feels like years have passed, my attention lands on the mantel.

On the stockings hanging above the fireplace.

I blow out a deep breath and run my fingertips over the delicate curve of Bellamy's cheek. Together, like we're meant to be.

A tiny flame of hope ignites inside me.

No more waiting. Tomorrow I'll work up the courage to tell her everything.

8

Bellamy

DECEMBER 22ND

SUNLIGHT WARMS MY CHEEK, SLOWLY PULLING ME from the deep, hazy edge of sleep.

I squint one eye open, smiling at the golden glow. Cozy like this, burritoed in thick quilts and blankets, I never want to move again.

It takes a moment for my mind to come online and register that I'm up in the loft.

How the hell did Hank get me up here?

An image of a sexy cowboy fireman-carrying me up the ladder floats through my mind, making my cheeks heat. Damn if that doesn't uproot the swoon in my heart.

Last night when Hank undressed me, I was so fixated on getting warm, staying alive that I didn't consider what we were doing. I got naked. With my ex. Worse, we almost kissed.

I don't know if that's first or third base.

And yet. There's no inevitable rise of regret.

Our closeness last night wasn't out of desperation or fear. It was out of ease, familiarity. My body, my heart knew what I wanted, and I drifted for that. Chasing his touch. His comfort.

Because that's what Hank's always been. Safety.

Oh God. What does he think?

No. It doesn't matter what he thinks.

He has his life. He's moved on. He's happy without me. I have to be happy without him.

Swallowing around the tightness in my throat, I sit up in bed. The gray sweatpants and oversized flannel I wear are soft against my skin. My hair a wild, ferocious mane of madness.

Though I hate to leave the warmth of the bed, better things are waiting for me. The scent of bacon wafts over me. And coffee. The best scents known to man. Or a hungry almost-crushed-by-a-Christmas-tree woman.

My sore muscles protest as I make my way down the ladder. At the bottom rung, I hop off, my feet hitting the hardwood floor.

Hank's bare chested and barefoot, standing at the stove with a dish towel slung over his broad shoulder. I smile at the crossword puzzle book resting beside his cup of coffee.

This is how it used to be. Hank in the kitchen. Slow, lazy mornings. Crossword puzzles and house projects. Tasks old people tend to, though we couldn't be happier to putter all day.

I'm tempted to sketch him. All his hard angles. That shock of messy brown hair, the way it curls at the nape. The serious, loveable man. In my anger, my pain, I forgot about the best parts of him. Charming. Confident. Strong. How could I have ever made that mistake?

He turns, his blue eyes searching my face with laser focus. "How do you feel?"

I step deeper into the kitchen. "Like I got run over by a…huh." I chuckle. "By a Christmas tree."

"Bellamy." He scowls like the reminder's personally offended him.

The skitter of claws snags my attention. Then Zelda is at my side, tongue hanging out of her mouth. Before she can jump up on me, I drop into a crouch and wrap my arms around her neck.

"I hope you gave her all the treats," I murmur as I bury my face in her scruff.

Brow arched in solidarity, he nods. "She woke up to the bacon-and-eggs fairy."

"Good." I steal a piece of bacon off the plate and toss it to the dog, getting in on the Zelda praise-fest. "Did you save Mama? Yes, you did. Yes, you did. Good job, sweet potato." With one more nuzzle against Zelda's scruff, I stand, evaluating Hank. "You look tired."

He flips off the burner, his voice strained. "Yeah, well, I couldn't exactly slip into a dreamless sleep after you almost died last night."

He moves to one side, abruptly reaching above me for plates. His hip, that deep V in his side, presses against my stomach. As he rummages in the cabinet, I stare at his abs, the scruff on his sharp jaw. God, he is one finely honed specimen of man.

"I made breakfast." He steps away. "You should eat."

"Caffeine first," I say, dazed, still inhaling his spiced scent.

Hank pours a cup and slides it toward me. "Here you go, sugar—" He flinches, catching himself.

My breath catches, my heart lurches. So that's what last night did. Opened us up. Sent us back. Oh God.

Blushing, he clears his throat. "Sugar in your coffee?"

I smile. "Nice catch." He knows it's always been black coffee or bust.

"Been on my toes since last night." He grins.

As he dishes a heaping plate of eggs and bacon for me, I stand at the counter and chew a nail. How many little slips have I almost had over the last three years? Picking up the phone, eager to tell him about my first art sale. Almost giving in to the urge to send him a raccoon meme I knew he'd love. Coming dangerously close to buying a beautiful old saddle at a thrift store for him.

He hands me the plate, but neither of us makes a move to sit. We eat standing up at the kitchen counter like heathens, staring at each other.

The silence grows, the only sound tree branches scratching at the exterior of the cabin. The sun shines brightly outside. The sky clear of snow and rain.

"Thanks, for, uh, you know." I swallow, my chest

tightening. "Doing the whole handsome cowboy rescue thing and saving me."

"I was scared." His voice is strangled, like the words stick in his throat. He tosses another piece of bacon to Zelda, who gleefully snaps it up. "I could have moved a fucking mountain last night," he grits out. "To get to you."

Breath hitching, I grip my fork tighter. "I was scared too. I was pretty certain there for a little while that I'd be crushed to death by a Christmas tree."

"Nah." He runs a hand through his hair, surveying me, then nods over my shoulder. "You both lived to fight another day."

I turn, following his gaze. Everything inside me lights up at the sight. I don't know how I missed it. Propped in the corner of the room, screwed into a tree stand, is the fluffy, fat Christmas tree of my dreams.

Delight and joy rush through me. Hand on my heart, I spin back around. "Hank. You got it."

"For you." He sets his plate in the sink, then leans back against the counter, considering me. "I acted like an asshole yesterday, Bell. I should have helped you." The tenderness in his words steals my breath.

I nod, his apology sinking into me like sunlight, and avert my focus to my plate. I scrape the remains of the eggs from one side to the other, looking for a fitting response. Looking for a way out of the old feelings suddenly sparking inside me.

Not old feelings, my brain whispers. *Because they were never really gone.*

"Blizzard's over," Hank rumbles.

I blink back to the present.

"I dug out the truck this morning. I'll pack up and head back to the ranch after I clean up the kitchen."

My stomach's a ball of nerves as he takes my plate, sets it in the sink beside his. He stands next to me, scraping eggs from the pan into the trash. This close, the heat from his body seeps into me. So does his scent. He smells like well-oiled leather and snow-drenched fir trees.

No. No. I don't want him to go.

My brain scrabbles for a way out of this lunacy. My body, instead, twists into him.

It's so easy to still think of him as mine.

So easy to wish he was.

"You should stay," I blurt out.

One dark eyebrow arches.

Heart in my throat, I go on. "It doesn't feel right to make you spend Christmas by yourself. Not after you expended all your body heat on me."

His deep chuckle vibrates through me. I shiver.

I shift against the counter, gripping it with sweaty palms. "You're here already, right? You might as well just spend Christmas at the cabin."

He doesn't respond, only searches my face.

"Please, Hank. Don't make me have a blue Christmas without you."

The pun doesn't land.

"Bell." He shakes his head slightly, his face drawn, agonized.

My hope plummets. It's what I thought. He doesn't want to be here. With me.

"You're right." I retreat a step, only to have the backs of my knees hit Zelda, who's hoovering the floor for scraps. "It's a dumb idea. You don't want to be here with me. I get it. I'm your ex. Why would you—"

"Bell." Hank's moved closer now. "Stop talking." There's the soft, calloused scrape of his palm on my cheek. For a second, I think he might strangle me. Instead, when his hand flexes against my jaw, a strange dizziness sweeps me up. My belly swoops at careful and hopeful angles.

He leans in, leans low, a stern seriousness tightening the line of his brow. And then, and then, and then—

His mouth is on mine.

Pressing hard. Inhaling my gasp. The man kisses me like he's starving. Maybe he is. Because I'm just as hungry.

My shaky hands wrap around his shoulders before sliding up his neck and into his hair. I burrow closer, almost a physical lunge of my lust.

We groan in unison. Our bodies two hot suns colliding, brilliant and burning.

We move together, frantically, hungrily. Like the last three years are a dam burst. Like we can reclaim the past. Like we remember each other's bodies. What we like. What we don't. What we need.

"Need you," he murmurs, pressing closer, hands on the elastic waistband of my sweatpants. Desperate and panting, he drags his sharp whiskers up the curve of my throat. I feel his shudder in my ear. His warm breath on my temple a moment before his lips meet mine once more.

It's a repeat of last night. Only this time, I don't want it to stop.

"It's been so long." I sift my hands in his hair and arch my hips, relishing his heavy thickness against me, his harsh intake of breath.

I wish my voice wasn't so desperate, so full of lust. But there's no room for embarrassment. Not when Hank's tone matches mine.

"I know, sugar." His groan vibrates through me.

Hands on his shoulders, I bite at his lush lower lip. Can't get enough of him. I want his body to melt into mine, to consume me. We kiss for an eternity, only breaking apart when we're breathless.

"Goddamn, Bluebell," he husks against my ear. "I missed you. Missed you so fucking much. Missed this." A kiss pressed to my cheek. "Missed you." His big hands inch my sweatpants down until they're a puddle at my feet. "Missed this gorgeous fucking pussy." One long finger dips inside me.

My heart rate skyrockets.

"Let's see, sugar. See if you still like this."

I whimper at how good it feels.

Hank grins. "That's what I thought. Still fucking aching for me, aren't you?"

Head lolling, I sigh. My dirty-talking cowboy with his hands of steel and velvet. I've never missed him more.

He steps into me, dropping his forehead to my shoulder, and scoops me up. His biceps flex as he places me on the counter. I wobble once, like a top, before steadying myself with my hands on his smooth shoulders.

I drink in his handsome face, the lust darkening his

eyes. A brief slash of worry buzzes under my skin. "Hank, should we—"

"Yes," he growls out, the possessiveness lighting me up inside. He straightens, arms braced on either side of me. "We should."

"Okay," I breathe, bracing my elbows on the counter, dazed.

He dips low, watchful, dragging my butt to the lip of the counter. Strong hands palm my knees, guiding them open. Goose bumps skitter across my skin when the cold air hits my thighs. But that chill's quickly swallowed up by Hank's warm mouth.

He buries his face between my legs and groans. "Tastes the same," he rasps, pulling back slightly. "Tastes like mine."

"Cowboy." I arch into the lazy swirls of his tongue, eyes falling closed. Desire pulses in my core. I haven't felt this way in a long time. So wanted. So desired.

Nothing has ever come close to Hank's madness for me.

A hoarse moan erupts from his throat. Good lord, the man devours me like he's starving.

He eats me until my limbs are limp and trembling, until I detonate, writhing against his mouth. I'm almost there. But Hank isn't.

"Don't come," he orders.

Undone, I laugh, groaning at the kitchen ceiling. "You better make it up to me."

"Damn straight." He nips gently at the inside of my thigh and pulls back, one of my legs still draped over his arm, to meet my eyes. He's looking for doubt, for regret.

But there is none.

I press myself up on my elbows and smile. "More, please," I say like I'm asking for another helping of dessert. Because that's exactly what this is. Delicious, sweet and endlessly enjoyable.

I'm greedy for him.

Adam's apple bobbing, he runs his hands up my thighs. Then, clutching my waist, he pulls me off the counter, into him.

I surge upward on tiptoes, fusing my lips to his.

We're fumbling and frantic. My shirt's off, then his jeans. Hank turns me, bends me over the counter, his big body curled possessively around me. My blood thrums as his hot, thick cock presses against my legs.

He plants a knee between my thighs, parting them. As he sinks into me, a strangled kind of sound erupts from his mouth.

Hank Blue whimpering.

Now I've heard everything.

"Christ, sugar." He snakes one big hand around me and cups my breast. Calloused fingertips pinching my nipple.

I nearly come undone at the sensation.

"Feel good, Bell? Just like that, right?" He plumps my breast in his palm, a rough grip I've always adored.

I gasp, one tiny mewl shamelessly slipping from my lips.

"That's right." A grunt, a thrust. "I remember what my girl likes. What you fucking need."

"Yes, yes," I whisper, lost in the healing sensation of him. Lost in us.

He drives deeper, one hand cupping the back of my neck gently. We moan together and thrust faster. He drops his mouth to my temple and whispers my name—*Bellamy, Bluebell*—as he moves in and out of my body.

I arch, head falling back against his sculpted chest. He cradles me to him, adjusting his position, sliding a hand over my belly. My body ignites into sparks.

Wanting more, I twist in his arms, kiss his scruffy cheek, the hard angle of his jaw. He locks me to him, his hand drifting to where we're joined, stroking over my clit. Smooth strokes, then rough. A rhythm my body's ravenous for.

"Hank," I gasp. The telltale vibration starts in my core. It travels the length of me as I rock my hips, chasing that over-the-edge feeling.

Our breaths echo in the kitchen. He watches me, never once breaking eye contact.

"Come." He rotates his finger and thrusts his hips. "Now."

Electricity tears through my body. Hank and I come together, shockwaves rippling between us. I catch a glimpse of his face, those deep wells of sapphire, as he shudders his release. My heart swells. He's so beautiful.

"So pretty," he husks against the shell of my ear. "So damn pretty when you come."

Gasping, I sag against the kitchen counter, hands splayed to steady myself.

With a groan, he drapes himself over me, languorously kissing up my spine, the curve of my shoulder, the shell of my ear. "Fuck," he breathes. The deep rumble of his voice, his heartbeat pound into me. "Goddamn, Bellamy. I missed this."

I missed it too.

I straighten, keeping that thought to myself, and shift in his arms to face him. But he keeps me trapped against his warm and heavy body.

With a sigh, I search his face. "Hank, this can't—"

He cuts me off with a demanding kiss.

The last thought that goes through my mind before he scoops me up in his arms isn't *I should get the hell out of here;* it's *finally, I'm back home with my cowboy.*

9

Hank

"W E'RE BACK ON THE GROUND."

"We are," I mumble into Bellamy's soft skin. We had sex twice more after our post-breakfast romp. Now we lay in a boneless and tangled heap on the rug in front of the fire.

I never want this to end. Never want her to leave my arms again.

She burrows deeper against me, her dark hair a wild halo around us.

Lazily, I trace a line up her arm. Kiss the scar on her bicep where she jumped out of a tree as a kid and impaled herself with a branch.

Outside, the sun is bright, the light blasting through the cabin windows. Like the blizzard never happened. In truth, I thank my goddamn lucky stars for that blizzard. It brought me closer to Bellamy.

There's still so much we haven't said. Words, explanations I need. But for now, this is enough. We have three more days to broach the rest.

With a small sigh, she lifts her dark head. The rest of her remains hidden beneath the blanket. "Cowboy, I think you made me sorer than the tree did."

"And I'm thinkin' you're more beautiful than I remember, Bell." With her puffy pink lips and glazed well-fucked eyes, looking away is impossible.

A blush creeps into her cheeks, making her even prettier. "You've always been a charmer, Hank Blue."

I shift, tracing her candy-apple cheek with my thumb. Study every detail of her perfect face. Those big brown eyes and soft voice melt my insides. This is Bellamy in all her beauty. "Been too damn long, if I say so myself."

"With who?" Amusement laces her voice. "Your ex-wife?"

"No. With anyone."

"Hank." She searches my expression with careful eyes, her small hand frozen on my chest. "You haven't been with anyone else?"

"Nah, sugar. I haven't." I chance a question that could kill me, unease seeping in. "What about you?"

She clears her throat, never looking away. "No."

Warmth blooms in my chest, a pleased sound rumbling out of me. It's what I fucking thought. She doesn't want anyone else either. We share a bond that can't be measured. We'll always come back to us, no matter how long it's been.

What would she say if she knew I still consider her my wife? Still consider her mine. Would she laugh? Squirm? Maybe try to leave? If she did, she wouldn't get far. Not this time.

She opens her mouth to respond, but she's cut off when Zelda bounds happily over the heap of blankets. She laughs as the dog licks her face in greeting, then she pulls her down into the blankets with her to rub her tummy.

Love, lust roar through me.

Goddamn, how has it been three years? There's not a chance in hell I lose her again. The earth could open up and drag her down, and I'd launch myself after her.

But I have to go slow. Hold myself together. If I rush or push, I'll scare her.

She sits up, the blanket barely covering her. Stretching out her arms, she lets out a big yawn. "We should probably make ourselves useful today."

I groan. Back to reality. Going out on the ranch is the last thing I want to do. I'd rather stay here with her.

With my hand on the curve of her back, I yank her to me. "What're you gonna do?"

"I can paint while you're out." Brows pinched, she worries her lip between her teeth. "Not that it'll be any good."

"Sugar, what are you talkin' about?" I run a hand up her smooth thigh.

"Nothing." She looks away, effectively ending the conversation, and zeroes in on the tree in the corner of the room. "I could decorate the tree. It's almost Christmas."

Which reminds me…I never gave her an answer about staying for Christmas. It's what I wanted. A second chance.

"Listen, Bell." I turn my face toward her.

The buzz of the walkie kills the mood.

"Sure could use your help, son. Snow's clearing and we got a few straggling customers."

With a deep breath out, I sit up. It's always busiest right before Christmas. Late planners. Unexpected holiday guests. But that's what the spirit of the season is all about.

Dread and sadness move through me. This'll be our last Christmas running the farm. It's time to admit that to myself. I'm all out of options.

"Can I go?" She slips on my shirt, a flash of flannel in my periphery. "And help?"

I frown. "You need to rest."

Her lips twist, her brows lifting. "Like we did all morning?"

"Damn it, Bell." She's got me there.

"Please, Hank. For old times' sake." She scoots closer, only stopping when she's in my lap, her warm legs wrapped around my waist. The steady thump of her heart beats against my chest. "Let me go." Her mouth moves to my throat, her touch draining me of my free will.

I smooth a hand down her hip and squeeze her ass. "Best get ready to work, sugar."

"I can barely move, Hank."

I sit back in the saddle of the snowmobile and glance over my shoulder at Bellamy. Her petite frame's swallowed by my overalls and a thick Carhartt jacket. A sparkly pom hat sits on top of her head, slipping low and mussing her hair.

"Deal with it." I grip the throttle, accelerating. If she's coming outside to work, she's gonna be warm. "And drink your hot cocoa."

"You're a cruel man." Despite the words, a small, happy sigh slips from her lips. As we ease slowly toward the tree farm, she loops her free arm around my waist and sips from her tumbler.

I like that sound. Her touch. Hell, I liked everything about this morning. I like her beside me. The sight of her beautiful smile. Showering together before we left. It was like old times.

I've spent so long hoping for this. Now I'm fucking terrified. Because what happens after Christmas? She goes back to San Francisco? Forgets this ever happened? I don't fucking think so.

A flash of red in the distance catches my eye. Grinning, I gun the snowmobile. When Bellamy squeals, her hand tightening just below my ribcage, I let out a chuckle. I bounce over a pile of snow, and soon, we're pulling up beside the big red barn.

I wait for her to climb off, then I follow, taking it all in. It's like the blizzard never happened. The sun shines bright. The snow is powdery and white, making the farm seem like the picture-perfect destination for the holidays.

And it is.

For three more days.

Townspeople are out in full force. The best kind of chaos. *Oohing* and *aahing* over trees. Lined up at the hot chocolate truck. Employees lift their hand to me, some going wide-eyed when they see Bellamy. By dinnertime, my ex-wife will be a hot topic of conversation in town.

Christ, how the hell am I gonna tell Bellamy the truth about this place? She loves this damn farm as much as I do.

When my father comes into view, dread curls in my gut. Thumbs hitched in his belt loops, he sidles toward us, bringing the familiar scent of pipe and apple cider with him. "You two survived the blizzard."

"And each other," Bellamy says half seriously, half amused.

I breathe out slowly through my nose. "Where do you need us, Pops?"

He grins like he knows what we've been up to. "We've got one last Christmas rush, son." His jovial expression dies, voice choking up. "Let's get to it."

My throat tightens in response.

An arm grips my bicep. Bellamy frowns up at me, questioning, curious.

I don't explain. All I want is to get through this. I look down at her. "This time, try to stay unburied."

She gives me a shove and sticks out her tongue, then she waddles away in the thick winter clothing I've put her in.

Chuckling, I head for a family wearing matching winter jackets. They surround a massive fir tree and point excitedly. I doubt their small Honda can haul it away, but that doesn't stop my chest from lighting up at the glee on their faces.

An hour later, I wave goodbye to Mr. and Mrs. Yeager, who own the bake shop in town, my gloves dirtier than when I arrived. I search the farm, the thick curtain of trees, for Bellamy. When I don't find her, I tug off my hat and run a hand through my hair.

"Hey, Pops," I call out. "Have you seen—" A hard icy ball slams into the back of my neck, cutting me off.

The giggle that comes after has me turning.

Bellamy stands near the red barn, small chunks of snow clinging to the fabric of her mittens.

She wiggles her brows. "Let your guard down, cowboy."

"Now you're gonna get it." Grinning, I dip down and scoop a handful of snow. I pop back up, packing it tight, only to be hit in the chest with another ball of snow.

I lob mine at her, and when it smacks into her thigh, she squeaks.

I take off after her, cold air rushing over me, bringing me to life. With another squeal, this one louder, she bolts. I catch her behind the barn, pressing her back against the red siding. Her cheeks are flushed, her nose a cute shade of pink. White snowflakes cling to her lashes. I pull her closer, inhaling messy chestnut hair. It smells like pine and coffee and burnt sugar.

"Caught you, sugar."

"Lucky me." She hums, a coy smile tugging at her lips.

A laugh busts out of me, straight from the chest, the heart.

Fuck but I haven't been this happy in a long time.

She curls her hands over my shoulders, her expression turning confused. "Hank," she breathes. "Is this bad? What we're doing?"

"What are we doin'?"

Her lips flatten in that familiar scold. "Hank."

"Is anyone else touchin' you like this?" I tip her chin up, nudge my hand to the back of her neck, run my fingers through the silky strands of her hair.

"No." Her sigh is sweet and sexy.

"Then there's nothin' wrong with it, baby." Far as I'm concerned, it's exactly right.

"But we're divorced." Worry, uncertainty flare in the depths of her amber eyes.

That can be changed.

"Does it matter?" When she's silent, I swallow. My heart's ready to beat itself out of my chest. "Listen, Bell. You asked me to stay for Christmas. Do you still want that?"

"Yes," she says. "I want it."

As long as you want me, you have me.

I catch her mouth with mine. Sighing, she melts into me and hungrily returns my kiss. She's soft and warm in my arms. Nothing has ever felt this sure.

When she pulls away, she scours the stalls. "Where are Billie Jean and Thriller?"

I flinch at the mention of my favorite buckskin quarter horses, but I school my features quickly. "Think Pops put 'em in the pasture."

Despite my even tone, my gut sinks. It's a lie, but how do I tell her we sold them in hopes of saving the farm and the cabin, only to find it still wasn't enough? It'll break her damn heart.

Her attention lingers on me like she knows I'm lying. Then, with a small shake of her head, she takes my hand and smiles. "C'mon. Let's get back to work."

Together, we head back to the large lot, hands hanging in the space between us, our fingers tangled. Halfway there, Bell stops abruptly, her hand dropping from mine. I pull up short, examine her. She stands frozen, her gaze on a family that's just pulled in.

When the man climbs out of the driver's side of the SUV, my heart sinks.

Fuck.

I haven't seen my best friend in two damn long years.

Clint slaps his hands on his jeans, his eyes going wide with surprise. "Shit, man, it's good to see you."

"You too."

"Miss you around Buck's."

The crunch of boots on snow is followed by the appearance of a woman dressed in a cardigan and leggings.

Clint's wife Laura rounds the hood of the SUV. Blond hair. Pretty blue eyes.

Clint and Laura were our partners at Tuesday night trivia at Buck's. Some of our best friends during our marriage. It took all I had to go to their wedding after Bellamy left. After that I was like a pulled thread, slowly unraveling. I stopped going to Buck's. Stopped hanging around with Clint. It was too painful.

And in Laura's arms, a pink-cheeked baby in a *My First Christmas* snowsuit.

My stomach drops. *It should have been us.* The bitter thought takes up residence in my brain.

"Hey, Clint." Bellamy's voice carries soft and clear behind me. "Laura."

"Bell, you're back." My friend looks from me to my ex-wife and back again, his lips parted in shock.

"Just for Christmas."

I tense. *Fuck. I have to tell her. Soon.*

Bellamy steps forward, eyes widening when she sees the baby. I watch her spine shift to steel, her lips twitching. "You had a baby, Clint? Never would have guessed."

He laughs. "You're tellin' me. I'd be better off raisin' kittens."

Bellamy smiles at him, at Laura. "Congratulations." She peers at the baby. "She's beautiful. What's her name?"

"Thanks." Laura beams. "This is Rosie."

"I think we have the perfect tree for you and Rosie." Bellamy gestures toward the path leading into the grove. "Why don't you take a look? We'll be right there."

I swallow hard as the trio walks away, pushing away the bitterness, the pain.

Then warmth as Bellamy slips her hand into mine and squeezes. Like she knows just how much that hurt. Like she knows just how much I need her touch.

10

Bellamy

AFTER SPENDING THE MORNING AT THE TREE FARM, Hank drops me off at the cabin, then heads out to feed the animals.

I do my best to stay busy. I make a fire. Crank the music to the loudest rock 'n' roll decibels known to man. Pull out my easel, paints and a canvas. I gear myself up for a marathon painting session. Instead, all I do is stare at the blank canvas. The bright pops of colors of the paints. I squeeze a tube, transfixed as red splatters all over the palette.

"Fuck."

Red. Snow. Footsteps. Mistletoe. Hank calling my name through the cabin.

Cool sweat rolls over my skin.

My chest tightens. I drop my brush onto the palette.

"Fuck." I suck in a painful breath.

I don't think I've been this insecure since I lost the baby. And I've never recovered. It bled into every part of my life. A little voice is always asking *Are you good enough? Can you do this? Or will it happen again?*

My confidence in myself, my relationship with Hank, my art and my body were thoroughly shaken.

I miss myself.

And maybe I miss Hank too.

I must. That would explain what the hell I'm doing.

Sleeping with my ex-husband.

My body aches where he touched me, as if it's reminding me of what I've gained these last few days. Which only confuses me more. It doesn't mean anything, does it? But earlier today, by the barn, the heat, the intention rolling off Hank almost convinced me we could go back to the way we used to be.

The longing in my stomach, the guilt—the emotions I've been hiding from for so long—threaten to break the surface.

I love him. Never stopped.

Yet I'm the villain in our story. I pushed Hank away because I felt like a failure. And in doing so, I pushed away the person who loved me most in this world. I did a fucked-up thing when I walked away without an explanation.

Why would he want me back? I left him cruelly. I lost our baby. How could he forgive me? Why should he?

I chew my lip and stare out the window. The sky is clear, the sun dropping below the horizon. It's late in the day to be feeding the animals.

He might not be my husband anymore, but I know Hank as well as I know myself. His ebbs and flows. He's brooding.

Seeing Clint with his daughter today was like salt in a wound. The devastated look on Hank's face stole my breath. My instinct was to comfort him. I could almost hear his thoughts.

That should have been us.

I pack up my paints and palettes. The cabin feels heavy and dark, so I decide to invoke some Christmas spirit. I hang the wreath, add a pop of mistletoe to the hook. The sprig Papa Blue pressed into my hand as Hank and I left the Christmas tree farm.

"For second chances," he whispered.

I stare at the floorboards. The darkened spot of hardwood. With shaking hands, I kneel and press a palm against the stain. "I'm sorry. I'm so sorry, baby."

A tear runs down my cheek as I stand. Then a brief, flickering sensation alights. Calm. Acceptance. It's gone just as quickly.

It doesn't feel right to decorate the tree without Hank, so I pad to the kitchen and pull out ingredients for Christmas cookies. My mom and I always have a marathon baking session a week or two before Christmas. Snickerdoodles, gingersnaps, sugar cookies. All fair game.

We make massive platters and deliver them to friends and neighbors. A tradition I continued when I married Hank. *Home is where the cookies are,* my mom always says, and she's right.

Midway through a bowl of sticky gingerbread dough, the door flies open with a thunderous bang. Zelda skitters inside, shaking snow from her fur.

Hank stands in the entryway, tugging off his gloves and jacket. Briefly, his gaze flicks upward, to the mistletoe, but he says nothing as he moves toward the kitchen.

"Cookies?" His brows slant as he takes off his cowboy hat and tosses it on the table.

I itch to wipe at the smudge of dirt on his cheek. Instead, I nod and flick my wrist, incorporating sugar, eggs and butter. "Cookies."

"Hell, Bell, you ain't got no music on." He pauses at the counter, flips on the radio.

I smile at the sweet gesture of solidarity. "Santa Claus is Coming to Town" by the Jackson Five blasts cheerily from the speakers.

"Thought you hated Christmas?" I arch a brow.

"Someone persuaded me otherwise." He pushes himself against me, warm and cold at the same time. Close enough to touch. Close enough to kiss.

Bad idea.

"What's on deck, sugar?" He looms over me, so tall, inspecting the batter in a lilac-colored bowl. He grips the edge of the counter near my hip with one big hand, the bright band of silver on his ring finger catching my eye.

He never took it off. He still wants us.

Panicked by the realization, I beat faster, frantically. "Only the classics. Sugar cookies. Snickerdoodles. Peanut butter."

"My favorite." His gravelly drawl sends shivers down my spine.

I know. I know they're his favorite. I made two extra batches. Oh God. Oh fuck.

"Here. Taste." Without thinking, I dip a finger in the peanut butter batter, then stick it into his mouth.

He blinks at me, shock rolling off him. Then, slowly, he sucks the batter from the tip of my finger.

I'm horrified. Frozen in place.

"Mmm. Tastes real good," he says with a smug little grin.

"Glad to hear it." My cheeks flush. Quickly, I move my hand back to the spoon.

Hank threads a finger through my belt loop and tugs.

A small noise escapes me. "You, uh, don't need to stand here supervising." I shove the bowl away, worried I'll overbeat it in my panic. "I am perfectly capable of baking cookies."

"Know you are." With a happy grunt, he twists closer to me. His hand, warm and steady, slips to the curve of my back. "Not supervisin'. Just want to be here with you."

I bite at my bottom lip and evaluate the chiseled angles of his face. His scruffy hair. The heated look in his eye. I don't know what to do with this. Or him. Every organ in my body sparks with life. I fear Hank Blue has elevated my emotional wellbeing. Like a soft-baked chocolate cookie. Or the perfect skin care routine.

There's this pull, this need between us. Like whatever we started last night, we can't stop.

I ache to give in. To surrender to it. To go back and go forward at the same time.

I'm spiraling, panicking, when the lights go out. The oven beeps, then goes dark. The radio dies a slow, warbly death.

"Shit." I lurch out of Hank's hold and stab the oven's ON button. "The power's out." I scan the bowls of cookie batter. "Now what do we do?"

Hank reaches past me to a shelf. Grinning, he snags a bottle of whiskey. "Looks like it's time to have ourselves a good ole-fashioned cowboy Christmas."

11

Bellamy

CANDLES CONSTELLATION AROUND THE LIVING ROOM. The fireplace roars and crackles. Christmas songs play on Hank's phone, the sound tinny but joyful. On the coffee table, picked over cheese and crackers and slices of salami. A devoured bowl of cookie batter. Half-empty mugs of hot toddies.

Now we've graduated to shots of whiskey.

Hank sits on the floor, back pressed against the couch. I lie lengthwise behind him on the cushions. Balanced on his bent knees is a *New York Times* crossword puzzle book. One big hand holds a pencil, the other absentmindedly strokes its way over Zelda's speckled belly as she snores lightly beside him.

"Gotta admit," he drawls, casting a longing glance at the coffee table. "Mice food was mighty satisfactory."

I scoff. "You can't fool me, Hank Blue. I saw the way you devoured that cheeseboard." I hover over his shoulder, staring at the grid of black and white squares. "Two across. Crow's call."

"Caw." He sips his whiskey, then passes it over his shoulder to me, even though I have my own glass.

"Easy." I rotate on the couch, fighting the urge to sniff his hair. To run my fingers through the tufts curled stubbornly at the nape.

The scratch of pencil against page. "Five down. Seven words. A holly jolly…"

"Holiday." I swallow down the rest of the whiskey, exhale a spiced breath in victory.

He nods his head. Then, scribbles it into the book with those long, calloused fingers. While he hunts for the next clue, I ease closer again. Like some freaky couch voyeur, I take in the crinkles at the corner of his eyes. The way he chews his lower lip. The dark whiskers trailing his sharp jaw.

I tell myself to stop looking at him. Tell myself to stop thinking about the million small things I once adored about Hank Blue. A cowboy who played chess and read Fitzgerald while also loving ice-cold PBRs, karaoke and bar fights on Saturday nights. Hank contained multitudes. I was sold. I was a goner.

Maybe I still am.

Needing an excuse to cool down, I sit up and hop off the couch. I pull the bottle of whiskey from the mantel and refill the glass.

Hank lifts his chin, eyes me. "You put up my stocking."

"C'mon, get out the bah humbugs." I giggle, the whiskey taking effect.

"No bah humbugs." He rumbles with a laugh. Then, more seriously, he adds, "Thanks. I'm glad you did."

Flushing, I force a shrug. "I was confident you'd stay."

His gaze maps me as I return to the couch, sitting up this time, hoping it'll keep me from giving in to the urge to huff his aftershave scent.

"Do you still do crosswords as often as you used to?" I ask, pulling my legs beneath me.

His broad shoulders stiffen. Without looking at me, he says, low and intimate, "No. I've never finished a crossword completely on my own."

"I haven't done trivia since I left." It comes out like a breathless confession.

This time, he turns, intense sapphire eyes locked on my face. "I can't do karaoke without you."

I swallow. I could go on. Confess all the things I've missed about being married to him. I miss waking up with him, miss the way he'd let me use his heat to warm my cold feet, miss the presence of the one person who just "got" me and loved me even when I was being grumpy and stubborn.

"Two clues left." He clears his throat, drops his attention to the crossword. "A mess or fiasco."

I sip my whiskey, considering the clue. "Shit show." I giggle at the thought, then moan. "Just like my career."

The leather couch gives a rubbery squeak as Hank peers back at me. "Somethin' tells me shit show won't be in the *New York Times*."

"Try trash fire."

"That's two words. It don't count." Rotating his lean body, he turns and slides his hand down between the leather seats. He grips my ass and pulls me toward him, only stopping when my knees hit his chest. As he inches forward, I open for him, giving him space to settle between my legs. He frowns at the pout on my face, rubbing a thumb over my lower lip. "What's this for, sugar?"

His sapphire eyes hold mine until, heart aching, I drop my gaze.

"Bell," he says firmly, warm palms curling around my thighs. "Talk to me."

I stare into the fire, wishing it'd burn the tears welling in my eyes. The pressure I've been ignoring returns, builds. My shoulders inch toward my ears and my heart lodges itself in my throat.

"I'm still working at the gallery as an assistant," I admit, chancing a look at him. The whiskey's making me honest. "I was a one-hit wonder. No one wants to buy my paintings. They suck, honestly."

"They don't suck."

"You have to say that."

"No, I don't. We're divorced, remember? I don't owe you anything. I'm sayin' that because it's the truth."

"Ever since…" I lick my lips, push on, my insides constricting with heartache. "Ever since I lost the baby, I can't paint. And when I do, I hate it. Every canvas, every color I pick feels wrong."

Pain creases his face, his voice a broken rasp. "I'm sorry, sugar."

"My agent thought coming up here would inspire me, but…I feel as lost as I did in San Francisco."

"Are you happy there?" he asks, a solemn grit to his voice I've never heard before.

I shrug a shoulder, tears burning hot behind my eyes. "For the last two years, I've felt like tinsel without its sparkle."

He doesn't say anything else. He doesn't need to. Just his presence is enough.

My skin warms as his hands land on my cheeks. I let my eyes flutter shut, my head lolling in his firm grip.

"Nothing worked out like I planned," I whisper. A tear slips down my face. "Nothing's the way I wanted."

I could add more to that. *Because I messed up. Because I miss Silverwood. Because I don't have you.*

His strong throat works. "It's not too late, Bell. For anything. For everything."

Suddenly, I feel very sober. I stare at Hank. He lingers in my space, handsome and earnest as the day I met him. My pulse speeds up. The smell of whiskey on his breath. The plaid of his flannel shirt, green and brown and tan. His golden-brown hair and the way it catches the light of the fire.

It's hard to steady my heartbeat, to quiet the way it thumps with a reminder. *My Cowboy. My Hank.*

With a trembling exhale, I press a hand to my mouth. "I drank too much."

"No, you didn't, but it's okay. C'mere." He moves in, bringing his whiskered cheek to mine, his hands slipping around my shoulders to pull me in for a bear crush of a hug. His weight, his calm cause my stomach to swoop in a delicious way.

"I like your hugs." I smile into his chest.

"I like givin' you hugs."

I slip my hands beneath the hem of his shirt, reveling in the feel of his smooth skin, the way his abs contract, that sharp suck of breath before he breathes easy, steadily. Then he's pulling back, but not away. His mouth finds mine and I'm kissing him, kissing him because I want to, kissing him because I have no choice.

Every minute we're together, he breaks off another piece of me. Our past has never felt closer. All the reasons we grew distant and selfish are overtaken by the million little reasons we fell in love.

"Bell." Chest heaving, Hank pulls back, a hunger darkening his eyes.

My breath staggers. He's looking at me like he wants me back, like I am still his, and he is still mine. Like what we used to have is still there.

I've never seen anything as beautiful as Hank Blue on the edge of losing it.

"Yes, yes." I nod and gulp and lunge for his lips.

My hands rake through his messy hair, and he responds with a pleased sound in the back of his throat. He breaks the kiss, urging my arms up and stripping me of my sweatshirt. Urging me down on the couch, climbing on top of me. We tangle together, a sync of heartbeats and hands. A rhythm we memorized as we fell in love, a rhythm we still have.

For tonight, at least.

12

Bellamy

DECEMBER 23RD

THE LOW GROWL OF ELECTRICITY CARRIES ON THE air, and the world starts back up again. Still drowsy with sleep, I lift my head. When I discover the warm, hard body curled around me, I sigh.

Once again, I'm waking up with Hank.

A four-letter word that means bad decisions.

Once we started last night, we couldn't stop. We started on the couch. We ended up in the shower and then the bed. I'm surprised I can still feel my legs.

One thing's for certain: I really need to stop sleeping with my ex-husband.

And yet I nuzzle closer, kissing the curve of his broad shoulder, the constellation of freckles there. He lies on his stomach, his head turned, arms curled beneath the pillows. A shock of golden-brown hair falls over his brow.

The man's too attractive for his own damn good.

This feels too right for *my* own damn good.

Waking up, limbs tangled. Weekends spent together. A partner who really understood me. That was Hank.

The thought hollows me out. Hurts my heart.

Could we get that back if we tried? Do we want to? Does he want to?

A war rages inside me. I want Hank. Yet do I deserve him?

I kiss the curve of his shoulder, then slip out of bed and change into leggings and a long sweater. "Mmm, don't go," he mumbles, eyes closed, broad hand patting the bed in an effort to find me.

"Tree time," I say, gripping the ladder. "I'll make coffee."

Downstairs, Zelda wriggles around me and paws at my leg. After a round of ear scratches, hugs and kisses, I pour her kibble in the chipped pie plate we use as a bowl. I make coffee, thanking the electricity gods for bestowing upon me the ability to caffeinate.

The morning sun has found its way into the cabin, casting brilliant rays through the windows.

Stepping close, I inspect the tree. Inhale the scent of pine and crisp snow. Even after my whole near-death experience, it's as pretty now as when I first saw it.

As I sip my coffee, I fluff the branches and spread them out to cover any holes. I fill the stand with water, then I drag out the box of Christmas decorations.

Even as I work, my mind's everywhere but on decorating. I don't know what Hank and I are doing. It feels right, but is it? I have to go back to San Francisco in three days. We're moving so fast, and we've made no promises. Who's to say this isn't just a friends-with-Christmas-benefits kind of deal?

But how do I tell Zelda goodbye again? And Papa Blue? I didn't expect to come back and fall in love with them all over again.

A noise behind me knocks me out of my wandering thoughts. I turn, finding Hank climbing down the ladder. He shuffles sleepily into the kitchen and pours a cup of coffee. His gray sweatpants sit low on his hips, his toned chest bare, golden skin on full display. Heat warms my ears when I note the bite mark on his neck, the happy trail that runs down his tan stomach.

Chuckling, he lifts the mug to his lips. "It's time?"

"It's time. Tomorrow's Christmas Eve. It has to be done today." Typically, I decorate my tree the week after Thanksgiving. Waiting this long is a travesty.

Crouching, I crack the lid on the plastic box. When I'm met with a snarl of Christmas lights, I groan.

"I can help." He pads toward me, but instead of moving for the box, he loops an arm around my waist and gathers me close.

"This isn't helping," I murmur as he sweeps his lips

against mine. Once again, Hank Blue's making me ignore all my responsibilities.

Ex-husband, dummy, my brain screams.

Let me be happy, retorts my heart.

Because with Hank, I always was.

"Looks like it's time to break out the tinsel." Surveying the boxes, he rubs his hands together.

I groan. "No tinsel."

He slips a hand into my hair, distracting me.

I nearly purr at the sensation. "Don't you need to be on the farm?"

"Nah, not today." His lips lift, though the smile is forced.

I stare up into those bright blue eyes. "Are you sure?"

His focus drifts to the Christmas tree, and he steps away. Pain and sorrow stain his handsome face. He's hiding something.

As he pretends to evaluate the tree, I chew on my bottom lip and replay Papa Blue's comment from yesterday.

"Hank?" I cock my head. "What did Papa Blue mean when he said 'One last Christmas rush'?"

He opens his mouth, snaps it closed again, like he's looking for the words.

I stare at him, an uneasiness moving through me.

He rolls his head to the side and meets my gaze. His face looks carved as stone. "We have to sell the tree farm."

"What?" I whisper, my throat constricting. "What are you talking about?"

He bows his head, runs a hand through his hair. "We owe back taxes. We've been working to pay it off, but if we can't get the money, the state's gonna auction the farm off after Christmas."

"But—but the mountain is yours. It's named after your family. You can't lose it."

"You can when you owe the government." A frustrated, bitter sound pushes past his lips. "The city changed our mailing address from a PO Box to a street, and we never got any of the bills."

"That's their fault, not yours."

"They don't care; they just want their money." His voice rises, not loud, but heated. Zelda barks in affirmation. "I've been tryin' to come up with it. I sold off the horses." His cheeks burn at the lie he told me. "My Bronco, some saddles, but…Pops won't let me sell the ranch house. And I sure as hell won't let him sell his."

"Oh my God." I press a trembling hand to my lips. If the tree farm sells, that means the cabin goes with it. "Why didn't you tell me?"

"It's not your problem, Bell," he says firmly. "Not anymore."

My eyes burn with hot, angry tears. Stubborn, idiotic man.

He's wrong.

He might be my ex-husband, but no one's more important than Papa Blue. Nothing means more to me than our Christmas tree farm.

I prop my hands on my hips, fire lighting through me. "Tough shit. I'm gonna make it my problem."

He laughs, probably amused by my indignation. "What are you gonna do, sugar, go down to the bank and break their legs?"

I pull my shoulders back, lift my chin. "I could."

"Bell, this ain't on you to fix. It's on me." Now he's unsmiling. Pacing. He rips another hand through his hair and this time keeps it there. His eyes are shiny, that jaw set. "And like fuckin' everything, I can't. I let him down. I fucked it all up."

He's speaking about his father, but the words are deeper. They're directed at everything, especially us.

My stomach drops. "How much do you owe?"

"Bell."

"Tell me, Hank." I clip the words out, stern. "Now."

"Twenty grand."

I gasp.

The strong lines of his shoulders tense. That muscled jaw flexes. Hank's always been the type to want to fix things. He always tried his damnedest to get my life right in .3 seconds, whether I was upset or hurt or just hangry. And if he couldn't, he'd find another solution.

It's got to be killing him that he can't fix this.

"What about a loan?" I ask.

"Can't get one," he murmurs. "Not when we owe back taxes."

"My money, then." I exhale a breath, clarity settling inside me.

He frowns, eyebrows slanted low.

"The money in our divorce settlement," I clarify. "It's exactly twenty grand."

"That's yours."

"No," I say quietly, moving toward him. "That was *ours.*"

"You need that."

"I don't. I haven't spent a penny of it. I-I—" *couldn't.* It's what I want to say, but instead, I stick with "I haven't."

His eyes haven't left me, but he doesn't respond.

"I was saving it for a rainy day," I urge. "And this is the rainiest."

His lips tug, deepening his scowl. "I can't accept that."

"Yes, you can. Don't be a stubborn, grumpy cowboy about this." I palm the sharp line of his whiskery jaw and guide his gaze to mine. "You need to take it, Hank. This farm is everything you love. I love it too." I stare up into his eyes, praying he hears the truth in my words. "You can't lose it."

His Adam's apple bobs as he swallows hard.

Denying him the chance to refuse, I drop my hand and tangle my fingers with his. "Please. Let me help you."

He chuckles, some of the light coming back into his eyes. "What about the tree?"

"Fuck the tree."

He laughs. "Now who's the scrooge?"

"C'mon." I tug on his arm. "The bank's open today, isn't it? Tomorrow it'll be too late." I pucker out my bottom lip. "It's our farm and we're going to save it."

His hands fall to my hips. A ragged breath shakes

his chest. He kisses me, relief on his handsome face. "Thank you."

My heart surges. I am alight with hunger and love and lust.

He kisses me again, squeezes my arm. "I'll call Pops." He steps back, patting his back pocket for his cell phone, then hustles for the kitchen.

Zelda looks at me like *you're screwed now*

I bite my lip, widening my eyes at her. "Don't I know it."

13

Hank

OUR FARM. SHE CALLED IT OUR FARM.

That thought wiggled its way through my head as Bellamy marched up to the bank and demanded to speak to someone. As she pulled out her purse and paid off our back taxes in their entirety.

Talk about a Christmas fucking miracle.

The merry jingle of bells follows us as we exit the bank. At the bottom of the steps out front, she stops and looks up at me. "There." She smiles. "Problem solved."

I grasp her hand and tangle our fingers. "Think that's the understatement of the century, sugar." In a single hour, she solved everything.

It makes my chest tight and my eyes burn. This glimpse of the determined, clever, driven woman I love. She saved the farm. There's no way I can ever repay her, but damn if I won't try.

"Thank you, Bluebell." I clear the emotion from my throat. "You don't know how much it means."

She hits me with that smile that goes straight to my heart. "No. I think I do."

There on the sidewalk, she launches into a little spin, laughing. I lift my arm, twirling, then pulling her into me.

"Blue Mountain Farm is saved." She cocks a brow. "In the nick of time too. No thanks to you, you mean ole secret-keeper."

I laugh, feeling lighter than I have in days. "This is like the squirrel. You got your way, and it tore up my shop, not to mention that damn saddle."

She bats her eyes. "I can't help it that I'm very, very persuasive."

"Try stubborn." The words leave me with a grumble, but I'm smiling.

"You wanna take a stroll?" I nod down the block, signaling to where garland and bows line Main Street. "For old times' sake?"

"Yeah." Her voice is breathless. "I do."

So we walk.

Silverwood is bustling, the late afternoon sun sinking, giving way to the winter chill. One last rush for last-minute shopping. One after another, the storefronts are decorated with colorful bulbs, and "Jingle Bells" pumps from the candy shop. We pop into Java Junkie for to-go coffees and pumpkin scones. We stop at a new kitchen store and browse, quietly wondering about the kind of person who needs all these damn gadgets.

When we step outside, ready to head for my truck, her gloved hand finds mine. Our breaths puff white in the chilly air as we wander. Apple cider spices the air. Locals lift their hands in greeting, and I find myself doing the same.

Since Bellamy left Silverwood, I've stayed away from our old haunts, only hitting up the hardware store and the grocer. Today, I'm seeing it fresh. And it feels like home.

Home.

My gaze lands on Bellamy, keeping pace beside me.

I still haven't told her how I feel. How I've felt for the last three years. Because once I do, once I ask her to stay, there's no going back.

She belongs to me. Yet an irrational fear plagues me, warning me that she might not agree. That in three days' time, she'll get back on a plane to San Francisco, and it'll be like the last seventy-two hours have been a dream.

I'm not prepared for that. In my mind, there's no going back. There's no me without her. She saved the farm, but if I need to leave it in order to be with her, then I will. Because she's given up more than enough for me.

"Hank, you coming?" She steps forward and turns, assessing me.

My breath catches at the sight. Backed by the blue sky, lit up in the late afternoon sun, she's stunning. Her white sweater and jacket have slipped, exposing one bare shoulder. Her dark hair is soft around her face and cascades down her back.

"You want to go out?" I nod at the bar across the street. Buck's. Next to the door, an animatronic Santa *ho-ho-hos* and waves a beer. "Grab an early dinner?"

Her eyes widen with surprise. But she nods, almost shyly, her bottom lip caught between her teeth. "Yeah. Okay."

Hand in hand, we cross Main Street. As I hold the door open for her, the scents of fried food and stale beer and sawdust hit us.

Bellamy inhales deep. "Missed that smell."

I take the place in and let out a low whistle.

Buck's Bar is decked out, floor to ceiling, for the holidays. Garland wrapped around the buck head over the bar. A North Pole sign over the jukebox. Bartenders in Santa hats pulling draughts in Santa-shaped steins. Twinkle lights strung from the ceiling.

"Damn. Buck didn't just deck the halls, he Griswolded the whole damn bar."

Bellamy lights up, joy radiating from her. She loves this. "Hank." She giggles, pointing. "Those elves-on-a-shelves are violating the liquor bottles."

Chuckling, I guide her toward an empty high-top.

"How do you feel?" she asks, those brown-gold eyes of hers searching my face. "About the farm?"

"Honestly, sugar, I fuckin' hate that I let you do that." It stings, letting another person step in. It's not the cowboy way. But I'm not so proud that I'd lose the farm.

"Accept it, cowboy, and buy me a drink." The stubborn tip of her chin makes me smile.

"You drive a hard bargain." I lift a hand, signal to the bartender. My eyes go to her. "Still like the amber?"

"You know it."

Once we've ordered, I reach across the table and grip her hand, feeling the pulse that beats in the soft pad of her palm. Can't resist the urge to touch her in public. Touch her like my wife.

She sucks in a breath but doesn't pull away. "Think we're taking *old times' sake* to a new level."

I hum, lower my head. "Ain't upset about that."

We watch each other. Like we're pushing this as far as it can go, like we're trying to figure it out on the sly.

The beer is dropped off by a waitress. A waitress I, unfortunately, recognize. *Fuck.*

"Hank Blue."

I rub a hand over my jaw. "Hey, Cynthia."

She peers over at Bellamy, pulls a few coasters from her apron and drops them on the table. "Been a while since you called me."

"Yeah. It has." Two years, in fact.

Bellamy tenses and sits up straight, squaring her shoulders.

I squeeze her hand, holding her attention, and her entire expression softens.

"Well…" Cynthia looks from me to Bell and back again. "I'll let you get back to your date." She saunters away, returning to the bar.

"She seems…nice." Bellamy grits her teeth.

I grin. "You jealous?" Won't lie. It makes me happy to see that fierce flare of fight in her eyes.

"Shut up. No." She takes a swig of her beer, breathes out, then blurts, "Who is she?"

"Went on a date with her a while back." I shake my head. Might as well get this out now. Move one step closer to the truth. "But she wasn't you. Not even close."

Bellamy's body becomes less tense as she considers my words.

"I dated too," she says.

It's my turn to go rigid, but I tamp down on the urge to act like a possessive asshole. No matter how much I want to.

"I hated it." One dark brow arched, she wraps her hand around her beer. "But for the record, this is not a date."

"Whole bar seems to think otherwise, sugar," I growl out, low and quiet.

She flushes, subtly surveying the folks nearby, discovering it's true. Every eye in the bar is on us. But I only see Bellamy. It feels so good to be this close to her, like she's mine.

Her slim fingers slip to rotate the silver band on my finger, her attention bouncing from it to my face. She studies me with an unreadable expression. "We met like this."

"We sure did." I shove a napkin her way. "Think you can draw me again?"

For a brief moment, hesitation creeps onto her beautiful face. Then it resets to determination, and she's digging a pencil out of her purse. Tongue quirking out of the side of her mouth, she sketches.

While she works, she hums. Soft. Sweet. Happy.

God, I miss that sound.

Finished, she slides her sketch across the bar.

"What do you think?" She props her chin in her hands and looks at me from beneath long lashes.

Damn, she's beautiful. She's always been beautiful, but this three-years-older version of her is incredibly sexy. Confident and put together and perfect. With her wild chestnut hair and rosy cheeks, she's as stunning as the day she ambushed me at my table, all brazen and beaming.

It's a quick sketch of me in profile, beer wrapped in my hand. "It's too fucking good, sugar." I lift it up, one soft napkin edge drooping. "You're gonna make it. And when you do, you're gonna be big."

"Sounds like you know everything, Hank Blue." She bites her lower lip to hide her smile.

I don't know everything, but I know my girl. How she likes to have a glass of ice-cold white wine and watch *Forensic Files*. How her tummy always hurts when she's worried. But never about herself. Always about someone else. How she does a little happy shimmy dance when she eats food she loves. How she never gives up, even when she's scared or doubts herself.

"But yeah, maybe you do know something." She takes a long sip of beer, tracing a fingernail over the sketch on the napkin.

"Tell me something *you* know." I skim my fingertips along the soft skin on the inside of her wrist. Just the touch, the feel, of her grounds me.

"I miss this town. This bar." She nods at a group of busybodies in a corner, their focus fixed solely on us. "Those stupid idiots too." Smiling, she props her chin in her palm and looks at me. "I forgot how to do this. Go out. Have fun."

A long exhale escapes me. "Me too."

Her eyes search mine, silently asking where I'm going with this.

So I chance it. "But it's better with you," I say. "It's always been better with you."

Her eyes widen and an audible exhale escapes her. "Hank…"

With each word, I inch closer to the truth. Will she let me in? Will she tell me why she left? Give me just one damn hint as to whether I can give her what she wants. Maybe I never did. Maybe that's why she left.

Only one thing's for certain. I'm scared out of my fucking mind that I'll lose her at the end of this.

The bells above the front door chime as it swings open, and on instinct, the two of us turn toward the sound.

Clint and Laura wander in hand in hand and claim a corner booth.

"Must be date night," Bellamy murmurs.

"Must be." I drain the rest of my beer. Set it down harder than I intend.

Their appearance is like a big bucket of water. A reminder that Bellamy's not mine. That we're still divorced and in less than three days she'll be on her way back to San Francisco.

Unless I do something about it.

"Listen, Bell—"

I'm cut off as the microphone on stage crackles with an announcement that trivia will begin shortly.

Bellamy breaks into a full grin. "Tuesday trivia. Things sure don't change in Silverwood." Her tone's wistful, if not a little sad.

Across the room, Clint zeroes in on me, one brow raised. With a bullshit gleam in his eye, he lifts his trivia sheet. Laura, face alight, waves a hand, gesturing wildly at their table.

I huff a laugh, scraping a hand over my jaw.

"We're being beckoned," Bellamy murmurs, an eager smile topping her words.

"What do you think?" I nod at Clint and Laura, who have now scrawled *SOS* on the back of their trivia sheet and are waving it in our direction. Unexpected nerves thrum through my veins. "Think you still got it in you? Old times' sake?"

Bellamy squares her shoulders, hiccups, then slugs down another sip of beer. "Always."

14

Hank

"HOLY SHIT, HANK." BELLAMY SHIVERS, STAMPING her fur-trimmed boots on the front porch. Her eyes are wide in the dark. "Find that damn key."

"Fuck, I'm tryin.'"

I pat my back pockets, well aware of Bell shivering next to me. Well aware of Zelda pressed against the window, howling her distress because we're not within petting distance.

"It's so cold," Bellamy moans. Her voice is raspy from screaming out trivia answers like a woman with a personal vendetta against losing. I forgot how competitive my girl could be. Damn if tonight wasn't one of the best nights I've had in a long time.

"Shit. Think I lost 'em." I cast a desperate look at the window, wondering how quickly I can bust it in.

"If we're stranded out here, you owe me partial custody of your coat."

"Get in here, Bluebell." I grin at her.

She's a little tipsy. A lot beautiful.

I open my jacket, and she edges closer with a giggle. Arms wrapped around my waist, face pressed to my chest, she stays there. Fits so goddamn perfectly in my arms that it steals my breath.

Her hands skim my back pockets, and then my front.

When her movements get more frantic, I chuckle. "If you're lookin' to do somethin', sugar, all you gotta do is ask," I say, my cock twitching in response to her touch.

She laughs out, "More body heat, huh?" She backs up a fraction but doesn't leave the warmth of my coat, patting herself down.

She makes a little squeak and pulls back to look at me, that lush lower lip rolled between her teeth.

"Don't kill me, Hank. I have them." She opens her hand to show me the flash of silver.

"Damn it, Bell." With a shake of my head, I snatch them from her. "Makin' me sweat, sugar."

"It's called keepin' you on your toes, cowboy," she teases earnestly.

I open the door and move to step inside.

Rather than hustle in like I expect, Bellamy grabs my arm, tugging me back. "No, wait. It's snowing."

I step back outside, turning so she's practically in my arms.

She leans back against me, resting her head on my chest. "It's so beautiful out. That perfect Montana night."

"It is." I hold her tight, close, ensuring every bit of her is pressed against me. Instead of looking up, I examine her pretty face, committing it, this moment, to memory. Dark lashes against the curve of her dusky cheeks. Her warmth, the way her hips tilt back to mold to mine. The rise and fall of her chest.

We stand in the darkness, holding each other as fat, fluffy flakes fall from the sky. In the distance, the howl of a coyote.

Bellamy shivers, I shiver, our breaths puff white, yet we make no move to go inside.

Wind gusts. A slight stirring sound above us snags my attention.

I glance up.

Mistletoe hangs from the star-shaped hook in the doorway. I haven't stood here with Bellamy since the day we lost the baby. I don't move. Neither does she. Grief pinches hard in the gut, but it's easier to breathe than it used to be.

"What do you think?" I clear my throat, my voice raspy.

She looks up, following my gaze with dark, wanting eyes. "It's been old times' sake all night," she says in a breathy, pleading tone. "Might as well."

I brush my hands over her hips, gripping them to turn her toward me. There's a rush of air from both our lungs as we face each other. She steps closer. Slender, light hands slide up my chest as she tilts her head back.

Leaning low, I frame her gorgeous face in my hands and press a kiss to her pouty lips. She tastes like whiskey, chocolate bitters and banana bread simple syrup from that last cocktail.

Uneven breaths pulse between us as we fight for control. Her mouth brushes over mine, her tongue caressing as she explores. I can't stop myself from deepening the kiss. From demanding more.

Whimpering, she loops her arms around my neck and twists her fingers in my hair. The air rushes from my lungs, beer and whiskey and Bellamy muddling my thoughts.

This woman consumes me. Can't eat, sleep or breathe without her on my mind.

Yanking her closer, I fasten my mouth to hers. I'm already unzipping her jacket when I kick open the door.

"We have got to decorate that tree," she mumbles as I walk her backward into the cabin, my lips still on hers.

"Tomorrow, sugar."

Zelda flies at us, but I gently shoo her away. Tonight, Bellamy's just mine.

Together, we navigate the darkness, weaving between furniture and boots until we come to a stop in front of the fire.

Bellamy breaks away, chest heaving, cheeks flushed. "Need you, Hank."

"Fuck, Bell." I moan her name like my life depends on it.

Because it does.

She walks out that door again, I won't survive it.

"Here," she gasps. "Here." Her cold hands fight with my belt buckle, frantic.

I chuckle. "Easy, sugar. You hungry?"

"Yes," she replies, voice breathy and fingers twisting in my belt loops, urging me on. "Hank. *Please.*"

"You first." I drop to one knee and tug off her boots. Back to standing, I strip her bare. Jeans and panties in one fell swoop. Then her shirt and bra.

The cabin is dark but aglow with blue moonlight spilling in from the windows. Still warm from today's earlier fire.

"So goddamn gorgeous." My greedy eyes drink her in. The full swell of her breasts. The curve of her hip and waist. That tumble of wild dark hair.

She steps into me, shivering. Runs her hands up my sides, taking my thermal with her.

I drop my hand, palming the inside of her bare thigh and squeeze. "Goddamn, Bell," I grit through my teeth when I find she's already wet. "Look at you, leaking just for me."

Her glazed eyes find mine. I back her up against the wall, my restraint splintering. Her body beneath mine is more than I can take.

She flashes me a coy little smile as she spreads her legs and aims that pussy right at me.

A pleased sound rumbles low in my chest. "Ain't she pretty?" I drag a finger through her folds, earning the smallest, sexiest moan.

Legs spread even wider, she tips her head back.

I grip my cock and guide it between her legs, pressing into her slow. Then I hook my hands beneath her knees and lift her up, up, up until she's braced against the wall.

I thrust hard.

"Oh, Hank." Her head falls back, amber eyes shuttering closed.

"Fuck, Bell, you feel so fucking good." I kiss the hollow of her throat, the pulse beating there. Her body shivers as her inner walls hug me tighter.

I moan, feeling fucking frantic. Out of control for this woman. I never want to be apart from her again.

She lifts her head, her dark gaze on mine, connecting us.

The sight of us joined, all the gorgeousness of Bellamy dripping around us, makes my atoms riot, sends my pulse skyrocketing. "Fuck."

This is it. This is everything.

Once in a lifetime.

Love. Sex. Friendship.

That's what Bellamy is. My wife.

She'll always be my wife.

"Watch." I growl the demand out. "Watch me slide into you."

Her breath comes faster as she bows her head.

I slide out, lingering at her entrance, and watch her face change. Desire, lust, sadness, joy.

"Look. Look how goddamn good we look together, sugar. Look at us. It's always been us."

"Oh." Her eyes flutter shut, then open, locking on me again. A single tear drips down her face. "Yes, *yes*."

At her words, I surge forward on a roar, thrusting hard, burying myself to the root. She cries out, nails scraping up my back.

"You're so fucking tight, Bell," I rasp against her throat, her pulse point. "You're so fucking mine."

"Always yours," she sobs, grinding her hips.

The room fills with hitched breaths and whimpered moans. The scent of sex, of Bellamy, inhabits my senses. I'm lost in her, lost in the woman who makes me feel everything.

I drive into her, my movements rough. The photo on the wall tilts. Zelda barks. Bellamy laughs, hushed and happy, as she runs her fingers over my shoulder blades.

"Can't. Won't. Lose you." The words lurch from my mouth in a strangled moan.

"I know," she says, voice hushed and tearful.

I kiss her, sliding my tongue across her lips, tasting her tears. Our bodies mold together, heartbeats becoming one, hips pounding harder, pushing her over the edge. She cries out. The sound echoes throughout the cabin.

She tenses as she comes. Her thighs tighten around me, her hold on my shoulder firm. She burrows her face in my neck, her noises spurring me on. One last quick thrust, and I come. I gasp my release into her throat, incapable of rational thought.

Holy fuck, this woman.

The air rushes from our lungs as we cling to one another, Bellamy's legs dangling limply on either side of me.

I gather her in my arms, flushed and panting, and carry

her to the couch where we collapse in a heap and tug the blankets over us.

She lifts her head from my chest. A strand of hair sticks to her flushed cheek. "That was—" She blinks, dazed, wondering. "Everything."

"Sure damn was, sugar." I sweep a slow kiss over her lips. Goddamn, I love this woman.

I need that second chance. Need it like I need the blood flowing through my veins.

Every little way she needs, I'll be there to love her. The way I wasn't before.

A happy sigh slips from her mouth as she curls into me once more. "Tomorrow's Christmas Eve," she whispers, drawing a picture only she can visualize across my chest with her fingertip. "We need pie."

"We'll have pie, Bluebell." And so much more. The entire cache of food I stockpiled, preparing to ambush her Christmas.

"We don't have presents."

"Don't need 'em." She's enough.

"I need to decorate the tree."

"We'll decorate the tree."

Anything else you want, I'll give it.

I secure the blanket around her slender shoulder, my heart a pounding beat in my chest, like a countdown clock for the rest of my life. Because tomorrow, when the sun rises, I have no intention of letting her go.

15

Hank

DECEMBER 24TH

AT THE SOUND OF BARE FEET PADDING ACROSS hardwood floor, I glance over my shoulder. Bellamy, sleepy eyed and messy haired, wearing an oversized Blue Mountain Tree Farm T-shirt and fuzzy socks, heads toward me. She's adorable as all hell.

And all fucking mine.

The thought is instant. Primal.

I'm a damn lucky man.

Zelda scrambles up for a pet, and Bellamy drops into a crouch, crooning sweet words and accepting sloppy kisses.

When Zelda's satisfied, Bellamy stands. "Okay, now

we really, really, really have to decorate the tree." She slips her arms around my waist.

Setting the spatula down, I press back into her.

Her warm breath pulses against my neck. "It's December twenty-fourth. Santa would consider it a crime. He'll arrest me."

"He takes you away from me, we're gonna have words." Twisting, I curl my body possessively around hers.

She peers up at me, eyes dark, and grips the front of my flannel. "Hank Blue, don't you dare try to fight Santa. You'll get coal for the rest of your life."

"Risk I'm willin' to take." I grin, kiss the tip of her nose. "You want breakfast?"

"Later." Wagging a finger, she moves for the living room. "I'm three-for-three with this tree, cowboy. No distractions."

"I'll help." I remove the last pancake from the pan, turn off the stove and follow her into the living room.

She stops in front of the tree, fluffing branches and taking it in with a sniper's gaze.

"Assume the position?" I ask with a knowing grin.

She wiggles her eyebrows. "You know it."

I lie on the floor, half under the tree, and get a grip on the base. Slowly, I spin it around.

"There's a hole back here," she says when I've made a quarter rotation. "So…to the left—no, the right." She paces around me, her socked feet making no noise.

Warmth grows in my chest. Bellamy's such an artist. No constraints. This part of her has always been my favorite. Goofy and free and happy, while I keep everything steady.

I give the tree another slow spin.

"A little more...stop...right...*there*." Her yelp of victory tells me I nailed it.

I pull myself up off the floor, grinning. From there, we fall into a routine so easy, it's hard to believe we haven't done this in three years. I dig the tree decorations out of tote bins while Bellamy, singing along to Christmas songs, decorates.

The Christmas lights go on first. She chooses white lights and, starting from the bottom, slowly winds them around the tree, working her way up.

She's busy fighting with the end of the strand when I step beside her.

She eyes me and groans. "Tinsel?" Despite her complaint, her lips twitch. "Hank. Be serious."

"Bluebell, it's Christmas. Have a little fun." I step close to the tree, tossing handfuls of tinsel over the branches.

Her squeal is ear-piercing. "Hank, no!"

I bark out a laugh. "The more undignified, the better."

Her lips flatten as she smothers a smile. "Fine. But one strand at a time."

Slowly, I circle the tree, covering it with tinsel until it's a shiny silver mess.

"It looks..." Propping her hands on her hips, she evaluates the evergreen with a scrunched nose.

"Goddamn gorgeous."

"Horrifying." Leaning into me, she gives me a kiss and

a warning. "You're gonna be the one to pull the tinsel out of Zelda's butt."

I dig out the tote bin full of ornaments and remove the bubble wrap from the one on top. Each one is a walk down memory lane.

The ocean wave carrying a starfish and a pair of flip-flops is first. Holding it up, I ask, "You remember this?"

She turns to look at me, a smile tipping her lips. "We got it on our honeymoon. Cabo."

Memories soar. Bellamy in a teeny bikini, salty skin and wavy hair. So many damn piña coladas, bad hangovers and bogarting the microphone at the karaoke bar until we were banned.

"I don't think we left the room more than twice." My mouth ticks up.

Flushing, she takes the ornament from me and hangs it high on a branch.

I smile as she *oohs* and *aahs* over each one. With each memory we unearth, it feels like we're moving another step closer to us. Keeping our holiday traditions, the roar of the fireplace, snow falling outside, Christmas music blasting from the speaker, Zelda nipping at our heels…

If I could keep only one memory from the last three years, this would be it.

I lift another bauble from the box, and Bellamy's chatter stops. I blink at the look on her face, the little furrow between her brows, then look at what I'm holding.

My stomach drops. It's the ornament she got me the Christmas she was pregnant. A mini framed photo of her sonogram. Beneath it the words *BABY BLUE.*

The decoration is tiny, yet it feels like it weighs a hundred pounds.

"Fuck." I take in her bright eyes, her pale face. "Sugar, I'm sorry." I didn't mean to do this. Make her sad.

"No." She steps forward, cupping it in her shaky hand. "Cody was a part of our life. We shouldn't forget him."

"You're right." I push the words out through my thick throat.

A wobbly nod of her head, at the small frame, at me. "You should hang it."

I do, choosing a sturdy branch at the front. With sweaty hands, I loop the twine over pine needles, arranging it gently, ensuring it isn't hidden.

Bellamy tilts her dark head as we step back to take in the tree. "It was hard, wasn't it? Seeing Clint with his baby."

"Yeah." I take a shaky breath. My fingertips graze hers, and she moves a fraction closer. "It was. Felt like it should have been us."

"He'd be four in April."

My heart thuds painfully. "I know."

Her voice comes out rushed, choked, as she says, "He was the best thing we ever did. And we were good together without him."

"We were." I drape an arm around her, pull her in.

She sighs, tipping her head to my shoulder. We hold each other in the warmth of the cabin. In the place we love. In the place that holds so much pain. This is the most we've ever talked about our son, about our loss. It feels like some kind of healing. It gives me hope that even though we'll never get over it, we can move on.

Bellamy sniffles, then wiggles her way out from under my arm. My hands itch to pull her back to me. To earn her softness, her warmth.

She wipes beneath her eyes, gives me a teary smile. "Well, that was cathartic." As she stacks up the totes, she says, "Maybe I can get some painting in before I go after all."

It takes a second for my brain to play catch-up, for her words to register.

Fuck.

With my heart in my throat, I ask, "Why do you? Have to go?"

She stays quiet for too long, her back to me. "Because of my job, Hank. Because of my life." A scoff pops out of her mouth, the slender line of her shoulders stiffening. "That's what people do when the holidays are over."

"When the holidays are over," I repeat, "but what about us?" My voice is raw with emotion. It's do or die. Tell her everything. Get some answers of my own.

"What about us?" She frowns, turning back to me.

"Bell. Don't do this." I swallow past the lump in my throat. "Don't pull away from me."

I step in front of her. She ducks her head, dropping her gaze from mine. She's trembling, her face a mask of pain. She doesn't want to do this. Talk about it. But we have to. Because I don't want her to go. How can I let her walk away again? The answer's obvious. I can't. I won't.

Bellamy doesn't get to play pretend. Not anymore. The spark between us, the tether are still there. I won't let her off the hook that easily.

She edges away, nerves creaking her voice. "We had some drinks. We had some fun. But that's all it can be."

"That's bullshit." I step closer, curling my fingers around her wrist to pull her toward me.

Eyes widening, she lets out a small gasping exhale. "What are you doing?"

"What I should have done three years ago." I slide my hand to her neck, my thumb caressing the high line of her cheekbone. "I still love you, Bell. I never goddamn stopped."

16

Bellamy

JOY HITS ME FIRST. THEN FEAR.

"Hank. You don't mean that." I laugh, a strange, strangled sound, despite the panic rushing through me.

"I do." His bright blue eyes are locked on my face. "I'm still in love with you, Bellamy."

"You're not. Being here is confusing. That's all." I shake my head, stepping out of his grasp.

My distance causes a little line to appear between his eyes.

"You, I mean."

"I'm not confused." His scoff sounds anguished. "I know what I want. I've known since the day you left."

"We're divorced."

"That doesn't matter." His voice is strained, frustrated. "You're my favorite person, Bell. There's never been anyone but you."

"Hank…" I swallow, my heart skipping. "I'm sorry if I gave you the wrong impression after last night…"

"That's exactly what I'm talkin' about. Last night." He bulldozes over my protest. "You felt it too. I know you did."

I did. That's why I'm terrified.

I love Hank, yes, but am I ready to do this again? What if we fail a second time? What if I lose him? I don't think I'll survive it.

"We had sex. Said things in the heat of the moment, things we didn't mean…"

"I meant them." Judging by the thunderous expression on his face, I've said the wrong thing. "You're tellin' me you didn't? You're tellin' me the last few days have meant nothing?"

My stomach drops and tears threaten. Blinking them back, I force my chin up. "They meant nothing because we're nothing."

"Bullshit." He storms closer. "You wanna do this? Pretend like you don't care, like you don't feel our connection when we both know it's a goddamn lie?" He lifts his hand, and I catch a flash of silver on his ring finger before it disappears to run through his golden-brown strands. "If you've stopped lovin' me, tell me that and I'll walk away. If I don't matter, just say it. If you don't care, then tell me."

I squeeze my eyes shut, the pain in his voice ricocheting through me. I can't be that cruel. But I can't have him either.

A dark laugh leaves his mouth. "Why'd you leave, Bell?"

My eyes snap open, snag on his. I'm trapped. He won't let me out of his hard gaze.

"I think I deserve a damn answer, don't you?" The anger in his voice claws at me.

My gaze launches to the sonogram ornament dangling on the tree. The Christmas lights blur as my vision swarms with tears.

How long before the worst thing in my life happens again? How long before I lose everything? How long before I fuck it all up?

At my silence, he shakes his head and takes a step closer. "You don't want to do this. You don't want to talk." His voice breaks. "That's how we got into this fuckin' mess in the first place."

He's right. Because of me.

"You need to move on." My voice wobbles even as I tell myself to be strong. To push.

"I can't," he says, the simple sentence torn from his chest.

"Why not?" I almost stamp my foot. Damn stubborn man.

"Because of you," he shouts.

The power of his words hits me like a freight train. I nearly stagger back.

"You. It's you, Bellamy. You stand in my way of lovin' anyone else. Of ever lovin' anyone else." The floorboards shake, and then I'm in his arms. "God, don't you fucking see that? Don't you fucking feel it?" He runs a broad, tan hand up my arm, and my body thrums in response. "Livin' without you every day feels wrong."

I want to echo his ache. I want to tell him the truth—*I didn't want to go; I left for you; I'm so damn sorry*—but I'm frozen in fear. So I say nothing. Instead, I blink at the Christmas lights as a hot pressure fills my eyes.

He sucks in a sharp breath. Irises sliced with silver, he releases me, steps back. "Fine. I get it."

"Hank." I reach for him, but he moves away. Regret eats me alive.

He whistles sharply and Zelda comes bounding. Sidestepping me, he strides for the door, hitting me with the chilliest of cold shoulders. "I'm goin' to the shop. I'll be here to talk when you're ready."

❄ ❄ ❄

I put the boxes away. Stoke the fire. Pour myself another cup of coffee and add a splash of Irish cream to numb the sad, hollow feeling inside me. Then I wander to the stove to clean up the breakfast we didn't eat.

"Fuck," I mutter when the scent registers. Hank made hazelnut pancakes. My favorite.

It's stuck in my mind. The devastated look on his face when I wouldn't talk. That's how we got here. Because of me.

Heart in my throat, I box up the pancakes and open the fridge. As I take in the contents beneath the bright fluorescent light, it all clicks. The amount of food in the fridge, my favorite things, the candles. It wasn't a mix-up, an accident, that Hank was here when I arrived.

He came for me. To get me to stay.

Hot tears fill my eyes.

I was a coward, a selfish jerk to let things get this far, to think these last few days wouldn't have mattered to him. Because they mattered to me. I felt alive. Happy. Whole.

Because before them, I wasn't whole. Not without Hank.

He was always there for me, matter how dark life got, and I wasn't there for him.

And now I've repeated the past. I pushed Hank away. Again.

He, on the other hand, poured his heart out, desperate to know why I left. Telling me he loved me.

I squeeze my eyes shut, hold my breath.

Oh. Oh no.

I've made a mess of things.

Especially myself. My heart.

I still love Hank. I never stopped. Not when I left. Not when I signed those papers. It was all an act to guard my heart. An effort to keep us from suffering more heartbreak.

I left.

And it was a mistake.

It's been clear since the second I walked away.

Hank deserves more than I've given him.

I need to move, to cope.

It's time to paint.

Once I've got music screaming from my phone, I open my bag, prop up the easel and position a canvas. Shoulders back, head high, I drag the brush across the canvas. Blood-iron red. Cornflower blue. Mustard yellow. Emotions flood me. No more numbing. No more denial.

Time to do the brave thing. And the brave thing is saying the scary thing. The brave thing is getting up after a fall. The brave thing is admitting to missing someone.

Admitting to still loving them even after all this time.

With emerald and brown paint, I add a craggy mountain range to the canvas. Slash a marigold sun in the bluebird sky. Wildflowers and nettles pepper the tall grass. Life rushes through the landscape, the scrape of the paintbrush like ice cracking over a thawing lake.

When I lay the paintbrush down, I step back and assess my work. It's not a neat landscape. It's a mess of gorgeous color, chaotic instead of calm. Misshapen, the elements almost bending against the canvas like they want to escape. But still, in that madness, in my art, I see what's there. An oasis. A home. A future.

A tear slips down my cheek. I don't stop it. Won't wipe it away.

Three years ago, we were both so lost in our own grief that we forgot to make room for anything else. When really, grief is love that has nowhere to go.

Love. All my life, it's either held me back or propelled me at rocket speed to what I want. There's no in-between. No indecision. Fear or certainty have always battled it out for the win.

And for the last three years, that's what I've been consumed with. Fear.

Because I lost my baby.

Because I loved Hank and left him anyway.

Because I didn't trust myself enough to heal.

It's my biggest regret. Letting my fear that it wouldn't work again get in the way of the happiness I deserve.

Still can.

Is our love worth the risk for a second time?

Eyes hot, throat tight, I stare at the beautiful Christmas tree. Every ornament Hank and I have ever owned, gifted to each other. Pieces of our life dangle delicately from thin branches.

That's life. That's love. Delicate. Tentative. One snap away from breaking. And yet we go on, we live the best we can.

Our hearts bloomed in this cabin, and they never wilted. Not even when we lost our baby or when we signed those papers.

Here, today, I don't have to solve my problems. Or fix my life. But I can fix what Hank and I have. It's never been broken. Just on pause. Delayed. Pushed down. But never forgotten.

I'll be here when you're ready, Hank's voice whispers.

Sometimes it's that simple. That little step forward. The determination to stop flinching when asked the truth. To stay when I want to run. To admit that I love him.

I exhale, a little spark of hope in my stomach. A sharp tug pulling me.

To Hank.

Time to be honest with him. Time to be honest with myself.

I inhale a steeling breath. Then I wrap a scarf around my neck, step into my boots, open the door and walk out into the snow.

17

Hank

"Christ." Breaths heaving out of me, I stalk around my workshop. I've been pacing since I left the cabin.

Bellamy stayed inside with her paints, cranking her music, working through what she needed to.

Just not with me.

She's scared, looking for a reason to leave again, a reason we won't work. But she's wrong. So damn wrong. She hasn't said the words, but I feel it. She never stopped loving me either. But fuck me, I don't know how to make her see it.

Time's ticking down and I'm in fucking agony. To love

her so damn bad and let her go a second time? If that's what she wants, fine. But I have to know for certain she's done with me before I'll let her go.

The creak of the door startles me.

I whip around, find Bellamy standing in the doorway in that oversized T-shirt, boots, bare legs and a scarf. Paint streaks across her cheek.

"Where's your damn jacket?" I bark, stomping toward her. I grab her arm and pull her inside. Then I shrug off my jacket and wrap it around her shoulders. "You tryin' to freeze to death twice this Christmas?"

Fire flares in her pretty amber eyes. "You came here for me." She jabs a finger in my chest. "You stole my Christmas on purpose."

Despite all the shit we've stirred up, I chuckle. "Took you long enough."

She opens her mouth to argue, but before she can utter a word, her attention drifts to the work bench.

"My painting." Her wide-eyed gaze swings to me. "You have it."

Marveling, she steps closer and runs her index finger over the edge of the canvas.

"I do." Sighing, I settle on a stool and rub my palms on the thighs of my jeans.

"How?" She worries her lip between her teeth, looking from it to me.

"I went to San Francisco," I say, shoulders falling. I'm caught. It's all out now.

She makes a kind of soft whimpered noise in the back of her throat.

"I came to bring you home. But when I saw you at your showing, hell, you looked so damn happy…" I swallow, threading a hand through my hair. "I couldn't do it."

A long silence. I'm crawling inside my skin, waiting for her reply, waiting for words that could break or save me.

"I wasn't happy," she bursts out. Her eyes are blurry. "I had a thousand texts written out to you that night. You were the one person I wanted there and…" She sucks in a trembling breath. "You were there after all."

"You were amazing that night, Bell."

"Why? Why didn't you say anything?" She meets my eyes with curiosity.

"I didn't want to take you away from your dream a second time."

"*You* were my dream, Hank. You." Her gaze drifts to the window, to the snow falling outside, to Zelda, back to me. A soft, sad smile tugs at her lips. "My dream was Montana and a cowboy and dive bars and Christmas trees and little blue heelers with overbites and skunk breath." She laughs, but then her brow furrows. "I never knew what my dream was until I got here…and it was hard as hell to walk away."

My pulse beats wildly at her confession. Hope pulls at my heart, breaths catching in my chest.

"Then why did you?" I reach out, snagging her fingertips.

Her warmth, her body, is so close I almost lose it.

"Why'd you leave? Was it somethin' I did, sugar? I know I wasn't perfect after we lost Cody, fuck, but—"

"No, it was nothing you did." Bottom lip quivering,

she hooks her index finger around mine. "You tried so, so hard, Hank. I'm the one who pushed you away."

A tear tracks down her pale cheek. I don't want her to cry. It kills me when she cries.

With a shake of my head, I tangle my fingers with hers and draw her closer.

"I'm sorry for leaving. For the way I acted. And I'm sorry—" A small sob escapes her. "I'm sorry we lost our baby."

"Don't." I close my eyes, pain clawing at me. "That wasn't your fault."

"It felt like it." She's crying in earnest now, wiping her face with trembling hands. "We wanted it so much, so bad…and I felt like I failed. Like I took it away from you."

"Baby, stop—"

"That's why I left. Because I was afraid. I was afraid it would happen again. I was afraid you'd end up hating me for it—"

I can't hear anymore. It's breaking my damn heart. I rip off the stool and crush her in my arms. If I don't, I'll lose my mind. She drops her head to my chest, weeping.

I kiss the crown of her dark head, stroking a hand down her silky hair. "Sugar, that was never your fault. Nothin' that happened was your fault."

The knowledge that she's blamed herself like this for so long tears me up inside. Because Bellamy's more than brave. And she's been carrying so much shame and guilt over a terrible thing that was never her fault. But I know now, and I won't let her suffer alone anymore.

"Shh, sugar. Don't cry. Please don't cry, Bell."

Clutching at the front of my tear-soaked flannel, she looks up. "And I did the worst thing. I let it break us. I forgot you were hurting too. I just felt so…empty, and I didn't want to put that on you. Even though I never stopped thinking of you. Even though I knew right away that I shouldn't have left. I fucked up. I fucked it all up."

Hand moving to her face, I run my thumb over her cheek to sweep away her tears. "It didn't break us. You didn't fuck up. We're standing here, ain't we?" I swallow past the lump lodged in my throat. "We got that second chance," I say, adrenaline pumping through me, hope and terror right along with it, "if you want it."

She gasps out a sob. "I want it. I want you, Hank." Tears stream down her face as she falls into me. "I'm still in love with you."

I lose it then. Every atom in my body comes alive.

"Fuck, baby," I rasp, crushing her in my arms. "I've been lost, Bellamy. Without you."

Three long years of dark turn to light the second my lips find hers. She kisses me back, frantic, furious, her hands in my hair. Salty tears stream down her pretty face. She groans, and I echo the sound as we lose ourselves in the kiss.

Love of my life. My bluebell. My girl. No more years between us, no more missing her.

Zelda, hating to be left out, barrels into us, nearly taking us down. She scampers around us, pawing at our legs and whimpering.

I blow out a shaky breath, stuck halfway between

disbelief and awe. I've spent so long craving this moment, hoping for it.

"Zelda," I laugh, peering down at my impatient dog. "I'll share her, just not right this minute."

With a smile and an exhale, Bellamy laughs. "I think she's happy."

"I'm pretty damn happy myself." I band my arms low around her hips and pull her close. "This life is too damn short to live it without you, sugar."

Eyes glittering with tears, she nods. "I'm a lucky girl, cowboy."

"I'm the fucking lucky one." I shake my head, lost in the moment, lost in us, me and her.

She leans into me, her lips ghosting over mine. "So what do we do now?"

Hands shaking, I cup her face, stare into her eyes. Getting to love this woman twice in my life is a goddamn miracle. But fuck, I'll take it.

I kiss her again, pull back, heart hammering. "Marry me all over again?"

Her eyes fill as she nods frantically.

I wipe at the stray tear that slides down her cheek. "That a yes, Bluebell?"

She smiles, wobbly but happy, and throws her arms around me. I rock her back and forth as she whispers into my neck, "It's a yes, cowboy."

18

Bellamy

DECEMBER 25TH

'M BONELESS. BATTERED. UTTERLY AND THOROUGHLY exhausted.

Not to mention, in love. After our confessions in Hank's shop, we retired to the bedroom and stayed there until morning. Now, bright sunlight streams through the window, warming my face. I lie on my back for a long second, basking in this picture-perfect Christmas morning.

This second chance.

I'm still so overwhelmed by the way this trip has turned out. Grateful too.

Hank's mine all over again.

I turn my head, finding Hank's sapphire eyes on me.

"Stare much?" I tease.

"Only at my wife."

A shiver works its way through me, leaving pure happiness in its wake.

The side of Hank's mouth kicks up, crinkling the corners of his eyes. "Happy birthday, sugar." He kisses me, arms circling me tight, and pulls me into his hard body.

"Hmm." I nuzzle into him, sweeping my lips over his neck, his chest. "Easy, cowboy. You're getting ahead of yourself."

"Hell, I'm aimin' to right that real quick, Bluebell." Brow furrowed, he sits up and checks the clock on the nightstand. "Think the courthouse is open?"

"Today's Christmas, Hank." With a laugh, I clutch his shoulder and drag him back down into the sheets with me. We face each other, wriggling together, my arms around his neck and his hands on my hips. "It's time for sloth and gluttony."

"My favorite sins." He rubs a thumb across my lips, his voice darkening as he says, "But there's nothing I love more than you."

"Hank…" I breathe out, my heart stumbling.

"I could stay like this all day. With you." The husk of his words vibrates along my bare skin as he inches closer.

"We have to keep traditions," I murmur.

He slips his fingers beneath the waistband of my silk sleep shorts, pulling a deep sigh from me. "Anyone ever tell you that you worry too much?"

"Only my husband."

"Sounds like a smart man." He nudges my cheek with his nose. "Tell me, Bluebell."

"Pies. Pumpkin. Pecan." I'm distracted now, a rambling incoherent woman thanks to Hank Blue. A calloused finger pressing on my thigh. I tip my knees open, the smallest whimper falling from my lips as he finds my heat.

"Horseback rides." Two thick fingers dip into me. I'm breathless now, eyes falling shut. "Coffee and Irish cream. Presents."

He uses the heel of his hand to work the delicate bundle of nerves.

I throw my head back, a shuddering breath leaving my lungs. "In no particular order."

"We'll have all that," Hank says, voice thick and throaty, "but first, a new tradition." He sweeps his lips against mine, the rough brush of his stubble catching my cheek as he pulls away.

I crack an eye, peer up at him.

Arms flexing, he presses himself up so he's hovering over me. His attention trails down my body, pauses on the dusky dark nipples peeking through my thin tank top.

Adrenaline and lust buzz through me. I straighten in the sheets, my body tight with anticipation, already arching, aching for his touch. "Better get to it, cowboy."

He gusts out a heavy breath, his bright blue eyes catching the early morning sun, all flecked with black and gold. "Goddamn, I love you, Bell."

I smile up at him, warmth building in my heart, in my limbs. "I love you too."

This is it. This is forever. I relish the moment. How he

exhales in relief when I tell him I love him. How his eyes soften. How he owns every part of me with just a smile. How he lowers himself down my body like he still remembers every curve, every scar.

"Can already tell…" Hank cracks a roguish grin as I drag my feet down his hips, sliding his boxers down. "This is gonna be the best damn tradition yet."

I shiver beneath his touch. "What? Naked cowboys on Christmas mornings?"

"Exactly, sugar." He lowers, bites gently at my nipple.

Slowly, slowly, he slides into me.

The breath rushes from my lungs in one wondrous sensation as love radiates through my entire body. Hank releases a groan from deep in his chest. Together, we're a mess of rocking hips. Bodies damp with sweat, frantic. Whispered I *love yous*. Eventually, we collapse in the tangled sheets. We're laughing, panting, as we reach for each other, his hand gripping my hip at the same time I wrap my legs around his.

"Bluebell," he whispers, pressing a kiss to the side of my head.

That simple name, that tone choke me up. There are no words to tell him what he's done.

Given everything back to me and more.

"I could have ridden my own horse, you know."

"But this is better." Hank's breath is warm on my neck as he leans in, pressing his front to my back. "Together."

"Yeah," I murmur with a smile, glancing down at his strong hand resting possessively on my thigh. "It is."

The pies are in the oven, and Hank and I are thoroughly bundled up for our Christmas morning horseback ride. Well, afternoon, thanks to our late start.

Moonshot, Hank's Tennessee walking horse, snorts as he leads her into a slow trot. We've brought provisions: a full thermos of coffee and hunks of Papa Blue's banana bread tucked into the saddlebag.

We're almost there. The winter chill feels like love. Electric. Shivering.

Ahead of us, Zelda gives three short yips, her universal signal for *hurry it up!* and blasts off across the snow-covered field.

"She thinks it's a race."

"She always thinks it's a race." Amusement in his voice, Hank snaps the reins.

Moonshot takes off into the breed's infamous running-walk.

We rush the remaining miles between the Christmas tree farm and the ranch. When we reach miles of white fencing, we take a left and crest the steep hill. At the top, the land evens out.

My breath catches when I see it. The house where Hank and I spent six years together. It's a small farmhouse with blue shutters and a wide front porch.

Happiness floods my soul so viciously I feel like I'll be swept away.

I swallow down the emotions that have taken over since I came to Silverwood. So big and beautiful over these last few days, I almost don't know what to do with them all.

Except I do.

I hold them. I let them in. Like sunlight through the cracks of an old farmhouse.

"What do you think, Bluebell?" Hank rasps, thumb stroking over the soft skin on the top of my hand.

It's not hard to decide what I want to do.

How could it be, when Hank is the easiest, the truest love I've ever had? This cowboy who's stitched my heart back together. Who encouraged me to feel everything even if I didn't want to.

I tip my head back to look up at him. His handsome face shielded in shadow by the brim of his hat.

"I think…" I inhale, and on the exhale, I say, "I'm ready to pack my bags and come home."

"Been waiting to hear you say that for three damn years now." He loops his arms around me and rests his chin on my shoulder.

On top of this hill, we take in the silence of the blue-hued Christmas Day. Snow swirls in the wind, but the bright sunlight cuts the chill.

It's bittersweet, having lost three years with Hank, but I'm a stronger, better woman because of it. I may not know everything, but I know what's important.

"We need to head back soon." I sink into his warm chest, savoring his touch. "Papa Blue will be over at three." And that means presents and pie. Eggnog and whiskey and Papa Blue singing along to Merle Haggard with Zelda as backup.

Hank hums low in his throat. He wants to stay here as much as I do.

That's when it hits me. I gasp.

He stiffens. "Sugar?"

I twist to look at him. "I don't have an ornament for you."

"I didn't get one either." He presses his lips to my messy hair and inhales. "Next year. We'll start fresh."

I shiver against the wind but smile at the promise in his words. *Next year.*

Whatever next year holds, I'm all in. Whatever it is, with Hank, I can handle it.

"What do you think?" His husky voice pulls me out of my happy thoughts. He lifts his chin, gesturing to the farmhouse, puffs of white breath billowing between us. "You want to go inside and get your ring?"

"You still have it?" I laugh, overcome with delight. Unexpected tears fill my eyes.

A smile tilts his lips. "My nightstand drawer, sugar. Been waitin' for you."

"Of course I want it."

Hank's smile grows bigger. He's so beautiful and he's mine, and I don't ever want this moment to end.

"I can't wait to love you again," he breathes against my skin as he tilts my mouth toward his and leans lower to kiss me. He tastes like maple syrup and smells like firewood.

Sighing, I close my eyes and curl up in his arms. "This is my favorite Christmas ever."

A rumble of a chuckle rolls through his chest. "And we got more to come."

"Promise?"

His voice, choked with emotion, is low and rough as he tightens his hold. "Yeah, sugar. I promise."

EPILOGUE

Bellamy

DECEMBER 24*TH* - ONE YEAR LATER

LIGHTS TWINKLE FROM THE CHRISTMAS TREE. THREE stockings hang on the fireplace mantel. Firelight illuminates Hank's tall, broad silhouette from behind. He sways slow and steady to a country song on the radio.

"You're being territorial." I set the tray filled with hot cocoa and whiskey on the coffee table. At the noise, Zelda *ruffs* and lifts her head from her dog bed.

My husband turns, grinning down at our one-month-old son, Jackson, cradled in his arms. "Ain't my fault he's already got me wrapped around his little finger." His voice is low and rough. It warms me all over.

All I can do is stare. I cannot get enough of my very precious little family.

"That so?" I step closer, head lifted, peering at the bundle in his arms.

"That's so." Hank's gaze lands on my face. "Same goes for his mama." Keeping one arm beneath the baby, he loops his other around my waist.

Sighing, I curl my body around him. We stand like that, entwined, slowly swaying to "Blue Christmas" in front of the fire.

Our son has tufts of dark hair, long lashes, rosy cheeks. He's precious and perfect and all ours. "Think he'll sleep through the night?"

A chuckle rumbles out of Hank. "It'd be a Christmas miracle." Those lines by his eyes crinkle. He's besotted.

So am I.

We got pregnant a month after we remarried. We were ecstatic. Then terrified.

There's no rulebook for losing a baby and getting pregnant again. For the first few months, I worried. To the point that I feared I was holding myself back from falling too deeply in love with what I could lose again.

But Hank was there. Through morning sickness and three-a.m. cravings and hormones, he never left my side. With each week that passed, with each doctor visit and flutter in my belly, I dropped the guards around my heart. I let myself be happy. Excited. Grateful. And when our son was born, I felt more at peace than I ever have.

Hank was my rock. My person. I appreciate and love him more every day.

I stare down at Jackson's sweet, sleeping face, his thick onesie studded with blue and red cowboy boots.

"He's the perfect gift."

Hank swallows, a sheen to his sapphire eyes. "He is."

Taking a step back, he carefully lays Jackson in the bassinet. Then he pulls me to his chest. "I want you to sit. Relax," he murmurs into the top of my messy hair.

"Hank." I pull back slightly, frown up at him. "You're fussing."

"I'm not." His look is entirely unamused. Serious, even.

Bullshit. The man has followed me everywhere since we came home from the hospital. He makes me sleep any moment I can, and he has taken over all midnight diaper changes and feedings.

If I could marry him again, I would.

"Who's coming tomorrow?" I murmur. In the firelight, my original wedding ring sparkles.

"Everyone," he says, grinning. "My dad, your mom. Clint and Laura and their kids."

I smile. We may have a full house now, but I still love our cozy nights where it's just the two—now three—of us.

"That means we should trade our ornaments tonight." I clap my hands, a thrill zipping through me. "Tradition."

With a nod, he guides me to the couch. He picks up a glass of whiskey and gives me a sip before taking his own. "You ready, Bluebell?"

"Oh, yes. Very."

Grinning, he pulls a bright-colored square from beneath the coffee table.

I laugh. It's a mini version of my painting titled *Cowboy's House*.

"For all your success this year." His voice is choked with emotion, pride in his eyes. "I'm so damn proud of you, Bell."

I'm proud of myself. Hank taught me it's never too late. I can chase my dreams anywhere; I only need confidence in myself. And a Montana cabin.

I clear my throat, my own voice warbling at the edges. "Thank you. It's perfect."

Our life over the past year has been a whirlwind. After marrying at the Silverwood courthouse the day after Christmas, I packed up my San Francisco apartment, quit my job and moved back home. I painted my heart out the second I got back, sold three paintings, and blew up on social media overnight, which led to an offer to display my work in a gallery in Bozeman.

When I'm not painting, I help Papa Blue and Hank with the tree farm. It's all been beyond my wildest dreams, but the cherry on top of our lives is Jackson.

I glance over at the bassinet where our son sleeps, then look up at my husband. "Ready for yours?"

"Lay it on me, sugar."

"It took a lot of work to acquire it," I tell him. "And I may have had some help from a very handsome gentleman."

Hank's face creases with a frown as I reach beneath the coffee table.

Finger looped through the silvery string, I lift the ornament.

As his gift comes into view, he lets out a loud exhale. His face, his shoulders soften as he surveys Jackson's tiny footprint, molded in clay. "Oh, sugar." His strong hand finds mine, warm, fingers curling around my own. "I love it."

"Should we do the honors?"

Together, we stand and shuffle to the tree. It's tall and spindly and is draped with multicolored lights and red ribbons. We went with Hank's traditional Christmas décor this year. I don't mind. It reminds me of childhood and is fitting for Jackson's first Christmas. Beneath the branches sit gifts of various sizes wrapped in plaid paper.

We hang our ornaments on the long branches of the tree, then step back to admire our collection. The ceramic dog figurine that represents Zelda. A tiny cast-iron skillet for our first camping trip together. When I find the silver frame with the sonogram inside it, tears blur my vision.

I'll never forget our first baby. He taught me so much. How grief and happiness are intertwined. How to be okay. How to mess up but fix things too.

Like he senses my melancholy, Hank wraps an arm around me and pulls me close. He kisses my hair, voice dropped to a whisper. "You okay?"

"I am." Twisting, I face him, hands on his broad chest. "Especially with you."

His smile speeds the beat of my heart.

"I love you, Bell." Hand moving to my cheek, he drops his forehead to mine.

"I love you too." I breathe him in. Cup his face. Kiss him deeply.

My entire being gets lost in Hank's steady presence. His heart. This man, this cowboy who has shown me that it's okay to be lost because he'll always find me.

Tiny, adorable snuffling noises come from Jackson's bassinet. Still tangled together, we tiptoe a few inches to the right and peer inside.

"He's dreaming."

Jackson's pouty lips turn up into a smile.

"That's what this feels like," Hank murmurs. "A dream."

"The best dream," I tell him, my body warming at the pure adoration in his expression. "One I never want to wake up from."

"Never been happier, Bell." He leans down and presses his lips against mine.

As I take in his handsome face, I wonder about all the Christmases we'll have together. All this love and the rest of our lives to do this over and over again.

I can't wait.

"How lucky are we?" I ask, my heart a hammer of happy inside my chest.

Hank holds me closer. "The luckiest." He brushes a kiss against my temple and whispers, "Merry Christmas, Bluebell."

I tilt my mouth up, sweeping my lips over his. "Merry Christmas."

My favorite time of the year.

All because of a cowboy.

Thank you for reading!

If you enjoyed the book, please consider leaving a review on Goodreads and the site you bought it from. Every review means the world to indie authors.

Don't miss out on Ava Hunter's upcoming books! Sign up at authoravahunter.com to be the first to get the latest book news and bonus content.

ACKNOWLEDGMENTS

Reader, I had a blast writing this novella. In fact, it was on my author bucket-list of items to check off, and now that it's done, it's time for my favorite part: the acknowledgements. Thank you to Ink by Kloe for the stunning cover. Beth at VB Edits for wrangling my words. Stacey at Champagne Design for making my pages pretty.

To my amazing beta readers: Jamie, Mary, Maggie, Megan, Jessi, thank you for giving your feedback to whip this book into its best shape. I love you all forever!

Lastly, thank YOU for reading this little Christmas novella! I'm so grateful to you for reading my words and supporting my author dream. I always say that I couldn't do it without you, and, well, it's true!

ABOUT THE AUTHOR

Ava Hunter is an Amazon top 50 bestselling author. She writes romance with heart, humor, and heat. Her bestselling books include Babymoon or Bust, an accidental pregnancy rom-com, and Tame the Heart, a grumpy/sunshine cowboy romance with Yellowstone-vibes. When she's not at her computer with a hot cup of coffee, you'll either find her reading the latest true crime book or traveling with her family. Otherwise, she'll be behind her desk, plotting out or typing up her next dreamy love story.

CONNECT WITH AVA:

WEBSITE: www.authoravahunter.com

NEWSLETTER: www.authoravahunter.com

FACEBOOK: facebook.com/authoravahunter

INSTAGRAM: instagram.com/authoravahunter

TIKTOK: tiktok.com/@authoravahunter